William A. Miles, Charles Stanhope

A Letter to Earl Stanhope

William A. Miles, Charles Stanhope

A Letter to Earl Stanhope

ISBN/EAN: 9783337091804

Printed in Europe, USA, Canada, Australia, Japan

Cover: Foto ©Andreas Hilbeck / pixelio.de

More available books at **www.hansebooks.com**

A

LETTER

TO

EARL STANHOPE,

FROM

MR. MILES.

WITH NOTES.

" Of all employments of the mind, furely that is the worthieſt, and as it
" were divine, which tends to eſtabliſh order in ſociety ; to humanize
" the great leviathan; to adapt the various parts of the vaſt machine of
" ſocial government, and nicely fit each ſpring where it can beſt act,
" each wheel where it can beſt move, to the purpoſes of the general com-
" bination ; to duly weigh and obviate the friction that might impede
" or ſwerve to the detriment of the diverſe parts, until the whole pro-
" ceed in juſt and invariable concert." Hiſtory of Athens, by Sir
William Young, chap. v. page 29.

LONDON:

PRINTED FOR G. NICOL, PALL-MALL; AND J. SEWELL,
CORNHILL.

1794.

ADVERTISEMENT.

THE number of faithlefs and ill-written narratives which have been given to the world as hiftories drawn from authentic documents, have long induced the Writer of the following Letter to wifh that the fcandalous combination between Bookfellers rapacious of gain and Scribblers without talents or principle could be expofed.

The licence which has been taken with the public credulity fince the Revolution in France excited the curiofity and created an intereft in the minds of men, is as unexampled as it is indecent; it calls loudly for reprehenfion, and ought to be difcouraged and if poffible fuppreffed, from motives of regard to juftice

and

and pofterity. The extreme avidity of all ranks and defcriptions of people to obtain information from any quarter, and almoft on any terms, was a temptation which even avarice with all its caution and circumfpection could not withftand. Hence the torrent of miferable compilations from newfpapers, and authorities ftill lefs refpectable, with which the country has been deluged, and which have been fold at a rate fo exorbitant, that the eafy unfufpecting generofity of the Public appears to have kept pace with the rapacity of thofe who have moft fhamefully abufed it, and who feem to think that every mode of acquiring money is honeft that is not penal. That character fhould be of little import in their eftimation may not be very extraordinary; but it is extremely fo that the patience of the Public fhould have fo long fubmitted to thefe fpeculations in

memoirs,

memoirs, hiftories, and correfpondence, and to thofe exactions which have turned out as profitable to the men who levied them, as they are indecent and difreputable.—If nothing however refulted from the folly of one party and the knavery of the other, than that of adminiftering to the wants of needy, or to the cupidity of mercenary men; this traffic, mean and contemptible as it is, would neither provoke notice nor deferve rebuke. But the evil is of wide and mifchievous extent, for the public mind has been vitiated and abufed by falfehoods as difgraceful to literature as they are offenfive to common fenfe; and it is this confideration which has decided the Author of the following pages to publifh, whenever his leifure will allow him, a variety of letters and papers relative to the different revolutions which have

have shaken with more or less violence every government in Europe, and which must have a very confiderable influence on the morals and manners of the rifing generation.

A refidence for many years on the Continent, and his having been a spectator of the revolutions in France, Brabant and Liege enable him to speak with certainty and precifion to a variety of facts imperfectly known in this country; and confidering his acquirements rather as a truft repofed in him than as the means of aggrandifement, he will not impofe fictions for truths, or trifle either with the impatience or credulity of the Public.—His object is to inform—not miflead —for every fpecies of deception is unfair, and fhould be reprobated. He means to inftruct—not infult—and as he is no lefs an enemy to defpotifm and every

abufe

abufe of power, than he is to anarchy,
he will deliver his fentiments with that
freedom and independence which cha-
racterife a mind ardent in its purfuits,
and paffionately attached to Liberty
and Truth.

A

LETTER

TO

EARL STANHOPE.

London, April 12, 1794.

MY LORD,

IF I have difpenfed with forms, I can plead the example of your Lordfhip; but the authority of precedents is fubordinate to that of reafon, and the occafion not only juftifies the irregularity of a public addrefs from a man who has not the honour of your acquaintance, but fuperfedes the neceffity of an excufe.

B   On

On topics of great public concern, in which the political rights of nations are no lefs involved than the civil rights of individuals, there is no impropriety in one member of fociety communicating his fentiments to another; and where the laws cannot reach a departure from the great line of duty which the Conftitution has prefcribed to men in high public ftations, the fupplemental aid of the prefs may be called for without any violation of that decorum and refpect which is due to minifterial or hereditary rank.

I do not mean to difpute but to remonftrate with your Lordfhip. The caufe of truth is feldom benefited by controverfy, nor is it always that error is corrected by invectives or perfonalities.

Occafions may indeed occur in which it is impoffible to avoid them; but they are in general the common refources of captious,

captious, little minds, and rather prove a vindictive and litigious difpofition, than a wifh to enforce conviction, or obtain reformation.

I difclaim fuch motives ; they are unworthy of the caufe I am called upon to defend, and as incompatible with liberal difcuffion as they are foreign to my temper and general habits. It is not conteft that I would provoke, but truth that I would demonftrate. It is not my intention to expofe the infirmities incident to our common nature, but to difplay in all their natural deformity the flagrant and audacious exceffes of that political turpitude which has of late mocked reproof, and infolently braved the anger and refentment of the nation.

Unaccuftomed to flatter, and naturally averfe to diffimulation, your Lordfhip muft excufe me if I fpeak in ftrong language — in a language fuitable to the

dignity

dignity of the fubject, and to that rank which I hold in the fcale of created beings ; nor can I, in difcuffing the important queftions under confideration, fail in the refpect which is due to your character, without forgetting what I owe to my own.

In confidering your Lordfhip as one of the hereditary guardians to whom the property, perfonal liberty, and the whole civil inheritance of your fellow-citizens are confided, I have a right to invefti- gate any part of your conduct that is likely to bring the facred depofits into hazard, which the laws have entrufted to your difcretion and integrity. It is on public, not on private ground, my Lord, that I mean to arraign your proceed- ings ; and if, from the appearance of your name in the title-page, Malevolence fhould indulge the mean hope of perufing a detail of private hiftory, in which the

the world can have little intereft or concern, they will be miferably difappointed
when they difcover that the following
pages are confined entirely to the tranf-
actions of the times, to great public
events, and to that line of conduct
which perfonal intereft as well as public duty prefcribe to your Lordfhip
in a language at once eloquent and
fublime, and infinitely more imperious
than it becomes me to adopt. It is in
fhort an appeal from the paffions to your
reafon; and in addreffing myfelf to your
judgment, I feel affured that you will on
reflection become fenfible of the mifchiefs
that may eventually refult to your rank,
character, and fortune, if the principles
you admire, and the doctrines you recommend, fhould ever be in a condition
to difpute the fovereignty of the laws, or
conteft an eftablifhment in the minds of
men with the milder and more equitable

maxims

maxims in which we have been educated.
It is thofe maxims, fo wife in their origin
and fo beneficial in their effects, which
it behoves us to maintain. We are not
called upon to fupport the miferable
views of party, but to refift the progrefs
of opinions deftructive of all order; it is
no longer a queftion whether the houfe
of Devon, or Portland, or of Lanfdown
fhall fetter and enflave both king and
people, and govern the country, but whether government itfelf fhall exift?

Interefts of far greater magnitude than
thofe which have hitherto divided, per-
plexed, and oppreffed us, are at iffue.
More important objects have fuperfeded
fuch confiderations—objects, my Lord,
which call on our vigour to fupport, and
on our affections to adopt and cherifh!
It is no longer demanded, which of the
factions fhall hold the fovereign and the
nation in difgraceful bondage, but whether

ther the fovereign and the nation fhall
exift? The defpicable reign of cabal,
thank Heaven, is no more ; and the people, relieved from the mifchiefs arifing
from low political intrigue, behold in triumph the ftupendous Coloffus, under
which even Majefty itfelf has been compelled to march with curbed neck, hurled
from its proud fummit and deftroyed !
It lies proftrate, my Lord; and would you
collect the broken and difperfed frag-
ments ? Would you, from its fcattered
parts form another whole, and, appro-
priating its powers to yourfelf, *compafs*
us and *lord* it over us, with giant ftride,
the Briffot, the Danton, or Roberfpierre
of the hour ? My Lord, there is danger in the attempt ; but if your courage
is equal to the enterprife, your honour
forbids it, for the infamy is greater than
the rifque. My Lord, the times demand
a firm and decided conduct ; and I tell

your

your Lordſhip, however Utopian the hope and Herculean the labour may appear, that the moment is rapidly advancing when Faction, that cut-purſe of the empire, muſt and ſhall be CRUSHED!

I am weary of recurring perpetually to the French Revolution—not that the ſubject is of a nature to be exhauſted, or that it can ever ceaſe to be intereſting ; but my ſenſibility is not equal to the taſk of contemplating with indifference the ſcenes I have beheld. The intimacy in which I have lived with ſome of the principal actors in that great event, the moſt of whom have been butchered or baniſhed ; the recollection that I have of Paris in its ſplendour, and of Paris in ruins and in blood, impreſs my afflicted mind with ſuch a train of awful, melancholy, and painful reflections, as to ſubſtract very conſiderably from the enjoyments

joyments of life, and to force me at times to regard the fpecies to which I belong with horror!

Yet while there are men weak or corrupt enough to hold forth the conduct of France as a model of fuperlative excellence, and worthy of imitation—while there are men fo little accuftomed to reflection, and of minds fo perverfe as to reject experience, and prefer conjecture to evidence; their guilt, folly, or obftinacy muft be oppofed by a force equal to that which they urge in fupport of opinions which fhould never have been revealed, and which ought to have been withheld, from motives infinitely fuperior to thofe which policy or perfonal convenience may dictate.

If the wife anfwer of Solon to the queftion which required a provifion againft injuftice had occurred to your Lordfhip,

Lordſhip, you would certainly have been lefs difpofed to recommend the proceed-.ings of men to our notice and admiration who feem refolved to do no right and take no wrong.

The only way to guard effectually againſt injury is " *by teaching ALL to feel the injuries done to EACH** ;" and with this maxim in view it is poffible that your Lordſhip would have a much bet-ter comprehenfion of your obligations to fociety, and much better underſtand the duties of a legiſlator, than by looking for a knowledge of either in the decrees of the Convention, or the fanguinary ha-rangues of ufurpers and impoſtors.

The conduct of France is recommended to us for imitation—But what have the French done, my Lord, but change from

---

* Hiſtory of Athens by Sir William Young, chap. v. page 31.

bad

bad to worfe ? Yet, deplorable as their condition is, that of ours would exceed it, if we fhould renounce the certainty we poffefs, to run after Utopian fchemes of equality, as ufelefs in fpeculation as they have been found dangerous in practice.

It cannot have efcaped your Lordfhip's obfervation, that the diftance from good to bad is much greater, and the confequences much more ferious, than from bad to worfe. Some degree of violence is neceffary to produce the one; but the mind anticipates the other, and is prepared for the event.

The moft moderate as well as the moft honeft men in France had long felt and acknowledged the neceffity of a reform. The abufes in the public adminiftration had accumulated to an extent which clogged the whole machine of government; and on a nearer infpection of

the

the evils that oppreffed and retarded its progrefs, it was difcovered that any thing fhort of a revolution would not correct the mifchiefs, or give fecurity to the nation for an equitable and provident government in future. The inftant the falutary meafure was propofed, a general ferment enfued; the entire nation fet up for reformers, and every one thought himfelf qualified for the arduous and complicated tafk. Unhappily for the public intereft and repofe, there were men who meant to go *farther*; and though they were clamorous only for *reform*, they had refolved on the deftruction of monarchy. We have alfo men of that defcription amongft us; artful and defigning men, my Lord, who bellow for *reform*, but mean REVOLT, and who would go any lengths rather than relinquifh their purpofe. The object of the new clubs and affociations which they introduced and

endeavoured

endeavoured to eftablifh in this country, was certainly meant to excite a ferment in the minds of the people: their object was to overawe Parliament and the Nation, and the tumult once begun, who can fay where it would end, whofe property would be fecure, or whofe life refpected?

Thefe are very ferious queftions, my Lord; queftions, which it behoves every man to confider, who has property to lofe or families to provide for, efpecially when they recollect that thefe commotions are exciting in the country by men who have nothing to lofe, and who are anxious to fee the whole empire blaze in one grand and comprehenfive ruin.

Do thefe men, my Lord, who look up to you as their chief, with for a total change in the government? If they do, what will that avail them? All well regulated governments, and I am fure

we

we will submit to no other, forbid riot and revolt. Do they wish for the destruction of monarchy? That is impossible, for the *thing* will exist though the *name* should be proscribed; and we know from experience that Protectors, Presidents, and Dictators have been more despotic than Kings. Besides, monarchy is our choice, not merely from habit or prejudice, but from a full conviction that it is a necessary ingredient in the Constitution. It is a *niche* that we have filled to prevent its being occupied by any one else, and our attachment to the throne is more the result of reason than of education. Is it the Peerage that distresses the dissatisfied gentlemen, who appear to us under such a variety of names that it would puzzle a host of special pleaders to describe them in a declaration? And is it in compliance with the clamours of such men that the House of Lords is to

be

be voted ufelefs? Is it in this country that turbulent and difcontented men would render titles as obnoxious and contemptible as they are on the continent, where vanity may purchafe a marquifate or a barony in an acre of furze, and fport the former after the other is burnt?

Is it becaufe the National Convention in France had the fervility to facrifice its honours to a mob, that diftinctions fhould be confounded and abolifhed in this country, where we know that they are conferred on men whofe virtues or whofe talents have benefited the State—whofe great and fplendid fervices have entitled them to honourable diftinction, and which, like an entailed eftate, defcends only to their eldeft fons? Where is the man who will prefume to fay that the titles conferred on the illuftrious names of Pitt, Thurlow, and Pratt—or on thofe of

Elliot

Elliot and Cornwallis—of Hawke and of Rodney—have been ill beſtowed?—What man, my Lord, but knows that the title of Mahon was conferred on the great grandfather of your Lordſhip, as a reward for his having added the iſland of Minorca to the Britiſh dominions; and that he was afterwards advanced in the peerage, as a reward for his ſervices in the cabinet? Is it not ſtrange, my Lord, that you ſhould be the only man that ſeems to have forgotten theſe circum-ſtances, ſo flattering to yourſelf and your family? Is it not ſtrange, that you ſhould wiſh to dry up the ſource from whence you derive both fame and fortune? Titles are ſaid to be conferred by the Sovereign; but it is, in fact, the Nation that confers them. Some perſon muſt be ſelected, in all ſtates, to expreſs the general will of the whole, and manage its intereſts—That perſon

in

in this country is the KING! and in whofe hands can the grand depofit of national honours and rewards be fo properly placed? It may therefore be faid in full confidence to thofe who would abolifh titles, and degrade great and good men, that while we efteem and reverence the peers in their legiflative and judicial capacities, we love them as gentlemen living amongft us, mixing cordially with us, and partaking of our diverfions. Look at them in the country, furrounded by an happy tenantry, diffufing mirth and plenty round their hofpitable manfions, giving employment to the induftrious poor, and animating, by their prefence, the whole neighbourhood! Drive them from their feats; profcribe their perfons and their very names; feize upon their property, my Lord, as the French have done, and what a ruthlefs fcene of devaftation will appear! God for-

C   give

give the man whofe cold and phlegmatic
temper will permit him even to contemplate fo general a ruin without horror,
much lefs to execute it! If the Peers, as
legiflators or as judges, abufed the confidence repofed in them—if, as men of
fplendid fortunes they infulted thofe
who were dependent on them—if, as
landlords they extorted from the poor
peafant more than the produce of the
foil he cultivates—or if, as citizens form-
ing equally with ourfelves a part of
this great nation their conduct was mean
or immoral—fome excufe might be offered for the clamour which thefe new
legiflators would excite, if poffible, againft
them. But the contrary of all thefe is
the fact: their decifions in parliament
have always been directed by wifdom and
equity; their general manners, in the more
focial walks of private life, prove that
fomething of more intrinfic value than

5   wealth

wealth is annexed to high birth. The
low rents at which in general their farms
are let, fome of which have been in the
families of the prefent occupiers for centuries, endear them as landlords to their
tenants; and as to their moral characters, in what body of men is there in
this or in any other country, more private
worth, more rectitude, or more good
fenfe? Why then are they to be deprived
of the rank to which they or their anceftors have been raifed by their merit?
What benefit can poffibly refult to the
nation from an act of fo much injuftice;
from an act that would deftroy that fpirit
of emulation, which we all know and
feel to be the fource at once of every
public and private virtue? As well may
we drive thofe great and refpectable law-
yers from the feats of juftice, which they
hold for our protection, fecurity, and advantage; as well may we degrade the

C 2   gallant

gallant admirals from the commands they have obtained for our advantage by long fervices, as to deprive them of the peerages conferred on them as rewards for the victories they have obtained over the enemies of their country.

Happily this queftion applies to every man in thefe kingdoms, where the road to places of truft and emolument, to wealth and diftinctions, lies open to the meaneft individual, and creates, as it were, a kind of emulation in the latter to acquire the former by honourable exertions or laudable induftry, an ambition between affluence and indigence. Let thefe excitements to glory be annihilated, my Lord, and this country will foon dwindle into that wretched impotence and infignificancy, which mark, more or lefs, every nation in the world, except the one to which you belong. What an excitement to talents and integrity in the law,—to

valour

valour at fea or in the field—to piety and virtue in the church !—Thefe three great avenues to the Britifh Peerage are open to *every* Britifh fubject; and not a man amongft us but may fee his fons or relatives advanced to hereditary honours, and his family ennobled; not owing to court favour, or to pecuniary means, but to the ftrong and triumphant claims of fuperlative merit, which, in this country, thank Heaven! can never be rejected. But if hereditary rank is offenfive to the felf-created friends of the people, what have the bifhops done to provoke their refentment? Their fees, with very few exceptions, are not more than fufficient for their decent fupport, and a very moderate provifion for their families.

No retrenchments that even parfimony itfelf could make, would be an object to the nation. Befides, the nation is pledged to fupport them; they are of our own

infti-

inftitution, and are become a part of the
conftitution. Their revenues are fo
many entails which defcend to their fuc-
ceffors, not to be touched but with great
delicacy, and not to be alienated but by
violent injuftice, What an infult to the
good fenfe and integrity of the country,
to fuppofe it will give the lie to its own
maxims and regulations, and barter its
honour for gain! Befides, it fhould be
recollected (and that with fome degree of
national pride) that a more learned body
of men does not exift; that their lives
are exemplary in the extreme; that moft
of them have been felected for their
merit, from the humbler walks in life;
and that their eftablifhment is fo intimately
blended with the whole hierarchy of the
church, that it cannot be feparated from it
without equal danger to religion and the
ftate.

Their diffolution would only be a pre-
lude to the deftruction of the inferior
clergy;

clergy; for it is the CHURCH, my Lord, and not the BISHOPS, againſt which all this artillery is levelled; and if the ruin of the one could be accompliſhed, that of the other would follow of courſe. It has been demonſtrated, that the entire produce of all the church lands and col-leges in the three kingdoms, would not divide amongſt the parochial clergy above one hundred pounds a-year; and as ſo ſmall a compenſation could not, conſiſt-ently with the juſtice and dignity of the nation, be offered in lieu of tithes, we ſhould loſe by their ſuppreſſion, eſpecially when it is recollected that a full fifth of them is in the hands of the laity, the private property of all ranks of people, and wholly unconnected with the clergy. But the objection that has been made to them, does not in fact proceed from a wiſh to eaſe the induſtrious farmer of what ſeditious and intereſted men would per-

ſuade

fuade him is a burthen; but from a rancorous and criminal hatred to all ecclefiaftical eftablifhments whatever. The Diffenters are a numerous, a learned, and certainly a very refpectable body of men; but they do not perceive that they are in danger of being made the tools and inftruments of faction. The abolition of epifcopacy would be followed by the fubverfion of prefbytery in Scotland, and of toleration in England. It is not the mitre and crofier that thefe *modern* reformers would demolifh. It is faith and good morals that they wifh to extirpate. Their aim is the general ruin and extinction of all religion; and the Diffenters, for aiding them in this diabolical enterprife, will only have the miferable confolation of being the laft facrificed. It is one of the maxims of bad men, my Lord, and from which they never even accidentally depart, to reduce the good to a

level

level with themfelves; and this will account for the indefatigable zeal with which committees were eftablifhed in France, and a correfpondence propofed by them, with the firebrands of all nations and complexions, for the diabolical purpofe of deftroying all thofe who had property or character to lofe, or who refufed to recommend a general infurrection and maffacre throughout the world. The unlettered African claims an equal fhare with the well-informed European in this infernal bufinefs; and in their nocturnal affemblies they feem to emulate each other in their indefatigable zeal for the extinction of all the virtues of the heart and mind. This is no random cenfure on an entire people, but a well-authenticated fact, to the truth of which many of your countrymen can bear ample teftimony.

My Lord, it is generofity—it is humanity,

manity, it is duty in your Lordſhip to undeceive thoſe well-meaning people who have been drawn into a wrong ſenſe of things by a ſet of enterpriſing and of courſe dangerous men, who appear to have abandoned the ſober callings by which they earned an honeſt livelihood, for the purpoſe, as they pretend, of correcting abuſes, inſtructing mankind, and eſtabliſhing what they call equal rights. That they have been ſo far deluded as to quit their former occupations, and ſo conceited as to run from county to county, and from village to village, preaching ſedition and revolt, muſt have been matter of deep and melancholy concern to their friends as well as of alarm to the magiſtrate. I am very far from recommending harſh meaſures, and equally ſo from believing them to be ſalutary. It is always well to commence by admonition, though it ſhould be neceſſary

perhaps

perhaps to finish by chaftifement. It would
be exacting too much, and being righteous
over much, to expect that men fhould
be angels: but though it would be abfurd
to require perfection, every man, on examining his own breaft, may find that they
can be better than they are. I am not of
that fullen and morofe temper that would
treat folly like vice, and whip it into fo-
briety and wifdom; yet, when any particular folly is artfully propagated, and
rendered as it were epidemical; when,
from being confined to a few obfcure individuals, fcarce known or refpected, it
is likely to infect the general mafs, and
become univerfal; when it threatens fuch
ferious mifchief and calamity to the community; it changes its very name and
nature, and ought to be oppofed by all
the force of reafon, and, if that fhould
fail, by all the force of coercion.

To fuffer it to grow into giant fize
without

without taking any fteps to crufh and extinguifh it in the bud, would be conniv-
ing at the infamy, and rendering ourfelves acceffaries to the guilt that deftroys
us. The phrenfy of an individual is of
little import—it can do little harm; its
duration is neceffarily fhort, and its mifchief of fmall extent ; but that of a mob
bids defiance to all eftimate, and propa-
gates itfelf by the terror it infpires.

As thefe itinerant legiflators, with
more rags to their backs than ideas in
their heads, have announced their plans
of operation in direct terms, it will not be
amifs to examine how far they are founded in wifdom, and likely to produce any
good purpofe; after which, it may be
ufeful to inquire how far fuch proceedings are juftified by neceffity, or warrant-
ed by the example of former times; and
finally, if they are compatible with the
general peace and felicity of civilized
                                    fociety.

fociety. In doing this, I wifh that full credit could be given for purity of intention in thofe who hold thefe new-fangled doctrines in porter-houfes, ale-houfes, cow-houfes, watch-houfes, and meeting-houfes; for we have patriots of all fizes, from dwarfs to giants; of all complections from pale white, to jaundice and jet black; and of all defcriptions from beggars who would be lords, to lords who are in a fair way of becoming beggars. Nay, we have them of all diforders, and with minds as diftempered as their carcafes.

Even the lame, the blind, and the paralytic are admitted into this chaos of reformers; and confidering the well-proportioned quantities of vice, poverty, and difeafe among them, it would puzzle juftice and humanity to decide whether this piebald affemblage of legiflators fhould be fent to an infirmary, or to an
houfe

houfe of correction. Wild and wicked, however, as their fchemes are confidered by all fober and rational people, I would neverthelefs fuppofe them totally innocent of every defign to fubvert the Confti-tution in Church and State, if they had not given unqueftionable proofs to the contrary; and confidering thefe brawlers not only as adventurers and incendiaries, but as enthufiafts and vifionaries, I will endeavour to convert them from error, by proving the abfurdity of *their* fears, and the injuftice of their complaints.

We have heard all the exifting regu-lations in fociety declared to be neither more nor lefs than a farrago of abufes, and that our anceftors were *knaves* for *devifing* them, and ourfelves *blockheads* for *fubmitting* to them. This is not the pro-per place to difpute to whom thefe epi-thets belong; whether to thofe who made and thofe who fubmit to thofe re-gulations,

gulations, or to thofe who would revile and deftroy them; but it is the proper place to ftate to you, my Lord, what thefe *well-informed* and *well-meaning* politicians call *abufes*, becaufe it will lead you to difcover, by implication, what they mean by PERFECTIONS. Among what thefe levellers call a blemifh in our Conftitution, and which they hold forth as incurably obnoxious, if not removed, is that of the executive power being placed in the hands of the Sovereign—not that they complain of the power having been abufed or perverted—not that they have any thing to alledge either againft the moral or political character of his Majefty, for in thefe inftances he is held to be exemplary, but that they deteft Kings and Monarchy, and would vote the deftruction of the former, and the univerfal diffolution of the latter, with as little remorfe as the fanguinary affaffins at

Paris

Paris murdered their fovereign. The executive power, they pretend, fhould be in the *multitude*, as it is in France, where every tree is a gibbet, and every other man you meet a hangman. I do not think that *fuch* a fyftem of government fuits your difpofition, and much lefs your convenience, or that it will ever be thought fo eligible as the one that we already poffefs. Nor do I think that pofterity at any period, however remote from the prefent time, will be difpofed to difcard royalty, and turn the nobility and gentry out of doors.

That fuch is the aim of our night-cellar ftatefmen, and fuch the tendency of all the writings and harangues fince the year 1789, cannot well be doubted; and if the portion of courage and good fenfe which abound in this country, did not form a barrier to this torrent of folly and iniquity, our fituation would foon be

as

as deplorable as that of our neighbours on the Continent. If mifma-
nagement, breach of truft, or any
other crime, had been alleged againft the
King, Lords, and Commons, fome reafon indeed would exift for *examining* into
their conduct, but *none* for *abolifhing* them:
and what other object this latter meafure
can have in the minds of thofe who propofe it but a general pillage, preceded or
followed perhaps by a general maffacre,
I cannot well conceive. This however
is certain, that fhould the clamour be
adopted, we would merit the reproach fo
often made us by foreigners, and prove
ourfelves to be as variable and as mutable
as the air we breathe: for what elfe
would it be, if, after all the hazards we
have encountered, all the blood we have
fpilt, and all the treafure we have ex-
haufted, we fhould refolve to level the
glorious edifice to the ground, which has

D been

been conftructed and erected with fo much difficulty, and under whofe fplendid and capacious dome we enjoy fo much folid comfort and fecurity? I do not know what others may think of this levity, fhould it ever happen; but this I know, my Lord, that were we to give into this phrenfy, we fhould fall into a worfe and more perilous ftate of flavery than that from which our anceftors fo bravely emancipated themfelves in the laft century, and we would become oppreffors, murderers, regicides, and fubverters of that which we have hitherto acknowledged to be *lawful* government, and to obtain which, an uninterrupted ftruggle for centuries has been carried on againft defpotifm.

I wifh all good and confcientious men to reflect ferioufly on the bleffings they enjoy at prefent, in this mild and happy country, and to imprefs on their uncor-

5   rupted

rupted minds this wholefome and indif-
putable truth, *that as every purpofe for
which men enter into fociety is anfwered under
a Conftitution where the* LIFE *and* PROPERTY
of the peafant are as fecure, and held as facred as thofe of a *Prince ; every idea of
abfolute perfettion in Government is chimerical,
and every affurance of its practicability not only
impudent and fraudulent in the extreme, but
dangerous to liften to.*

I do not addrefs myfelf on this occafion folely to your Lordfhip, or to thofe
who fteer their confciences by the occafion, and cannot lofe the honour they
never had; but to the honeft and induftrious farmer and manufacturer, who
denying vice and virtue to be mere relative terms, allow them to have an exiftence in nature, and believe the practice
of the latter to be as effential to their
well-being hereafter, as that of the for-

mer

mer is known to be ruinous to their happinefs and characters in this life.

Let thofe who pretend to have difcovered fo much imperfection and injuftice
in our laws, point out where they bear
hard on the guiltlefs and undeferving;
or where they are infufficient, except in
not being able to bring thofe to the whip-
ping-poft who libel their excellence, or
preach their deftruction.

To countenance the clamours of fuch
men would be contending for fhame as
well as fervitude, and reducing ourfelves
to the worft kind of flavery.

It would be carrying our ears to be
bored by men without names, and in-
verting the very order of fervitude, by
fubjecting ourfelves to the tyranny of
our fervants. Whatever may be the fentiments of thofe into whofe hands this
Letter may chance to tumble, I am fure

it

it will be favourably read by fome, and patiently perufed by all; for thofe that are againft innovation and licentioufnefs, will certainly be glad to find others of the fame opinion as themfelves; and thofe who are for riot and anarchy, have given evidence enough that there is nothing in nature which they cannot endure. Let the former of thefe be confirmed and fortified, by this Addrefs to your Lord-fhip, in their love of order; and let the latter take fhame to themfelves, if they can, for wifhing to difturb it. I am convinced that we fhall never be fo far humbled in fpirit, or degraded in morals, to receive the ignominy and affront that bad men would offer us. Having nothing to fay againft the particular conduct of any of the three branches of the Legiflature, they object to them in the grofs, and are for annihilating all of them at one ftroke.

D 3

But

But what do they offer to give us in exchange for the *King* whom they would banish, for the *House of Lords* whom they would abolish, and for the *Commons* whom they would dismiss with as little ceremony and good manners as they would their Sovereign?

Aristocracy more than monarchy is their aversion, and I do not well see how they can approve of a Republic, since it is *legislation* that they dislike and fear. It is not *freedom* but FREE QUARTER and FREE BOOTY that they seek, and when you consider the *no worth*, the *no quality*, and *no consciences* of these modern reformers, we are puzzled which to condemn; the arrogance of their pretensions, or the extent of our forbearance. How far such men are qualified to judge of abuses' in *any* state may well be questioned; but no doubt can remain as to the right they would

would affume to dictate to their fuperiors, and fuperfede the whole legiflative authority of the country.

If this fhould ever unfortunately happen; if men, the moft part of whom are beggars and malefactors, and only known by the villanies and mifchiefs they have committed, fhould carry their infernal projects into fuccefsful execution, our anceftors will have vindicated the liberties of England in vain, and have oppofed arbitrary power to little purpofe, fince in that cafe we fhould fall under the vileft of all defpotifm, and be governed by a rod of iron, without any other law or rule but that which the caprice of a ferocious and fluctuating mob, with as many minds as there may be individuals in it, fhall dictate. All kind of flavery, my Lord, is mifery; but that which is impofed by thofe who are themfelves objects of contempt and fcorn, and which is ac-

com-

companied by contempt and fcorn, muft furely ftir every honeft man's indignation, and is endured by none whom Nature did not intend as flaves. It is not meant to revile any man for his property, or for the meannefs of his birth; no blame can in juftice be laid on men for the faults of fortune, any otherwife than they make them their own; and if the poverty of thefe cellar ftatefmen is objected to them, it is becaufe it is accompanied with fraud and violence; and if I remind your Lordfhip of the quality of thofe whom you would *lead* to-day and may be com-pelled to *follow* to-morrow, it is becaufe they feem to have forgotten it.

In fhort, they labour to undo in an in-ftant what our anceftors have been work-ing for ages to acquire. They object to the *King*, becaufe it is his duty to preferve the public tranquillity, and enforce obe-dience to the laws—they object to the

Nobility,

Nobility, becaufe diftinction always implies fuperiority of virtue and of talent, as well as of fortune, and it is natural that bad men fhould abominate whatever brings to their recollection a fenfe of their own unworthinefs—they object to *laws,* becaufe the penalty of violating them is a reftraint on their neceffities and propenfities, and reduces them to the painful obligation of earning their daily bread by honeft induftry, when they could fupport themfelves with much lefs trouble, and in a much better ftyle, by *thieving* or *begging* if the *laws* were deftroyed : hence their quarrel to the *King,* and to the *Houfe of Peers*; they wifh to annihilate the authority of the *one,* in the hope of becoming ftewards in *truft,* and finally proprietors *in fee,* of the eftates of the *other*; for which purpofe they hired a man to cry down majefty and nobility among us, as burthenfome and difgraceful—

2

ful—But which, let me afk, in the name of common fenfe and of common ho-nefty (if *fuch* authorities may be appealed to without offence to your Lordfhip) is the more fo, a filthy fet of raggamuffins, riding lords paramount over the whole nation, levying contributions at will, inflicting death at random and at pleafure on thofe whom they meet or diflike, or an ancient and dignified eftablifhment, which, collecting as it were into one common focus all the fcattered rays of national grandeur, diffufes light, fplendour, and power, throughout the whole empire? I will not infult your good fenfe, my Lord, by preffing for an anfwer to this queftion, but merely remind you, that thefe halfpenny club politicians feem to have forgotten, that it has been hitherto ufual in thofe who hold great employments, to poffefs fome portion of integrity as well as fome degree of talent.

To

To judge according to the dictates of reafon, one would certainly imagine fome
fmall faculties and endowments to be requifite in thofe who would form or new
model a ftate; for though France has
ftruck off into a road hitherto unex-
plored, and the direct contrary to this,
though fhe has elected her Secretaries of
State, her Lords of the Treafury, Chancellors of the Exchequer, Judges, Admirals, and Generals, together with Priefts,
Bifhops, and Hangmen, from one promifcuous group of coblers, taylors, and tin-
kers, hungry attornies, and police men;
yet her example, I truft, will be no rule
or guide for our conduct in any one in-
ftance, and efpecially as thefe new Secretaries, new Chancellors, new Generals,
Judges, and Bifhops, appear to manage
matters but badly; and of all the new
arrangements (for appointments they
cannot be called) the *hangman* alone feems

to

to have *executed* his office with *effect*. I
fhould not have faid fo much in this place
of the affairs of that country, although
they have been held out as a pattern for
us to follow in this, if I had not wifhed
your Lordfhip to recollect, that the talents requifite for the higher departments
are not ufually acquired in fhops, ftalls,
or prifons, or caught by following the
plough. What *other* academies thofe
have been bred in, who *infift* fo vocife-
roufly on *reforming* and *governing* of us, I
know not, or what other arts they have
been verfed in, except thofe that require
good arms and good fhoulders rather than
good heads ; but this I know, that as we
would not willingly commit the education of our children to ignorant and illi-
terate mafters, or the management even
of our horfes to unfkilful grooms, it is incumbent on us to have fome regard into
whofe hands we commit the management
of

of the commonwealth ; and that if we will not have perfons of diftinguifhed rank and fortune to be our rulers, who are the leaft likely to play us foul as we have the greateft ftake at hazard, it behoves us, for our own credit and fafety, to have men of parts and education, in whofe abilities and judgment we may venture to confide, and whofe known integrity will fecure our property from wafte or depredation.

In fhort, it is our duty, and I am fure it is our intereft, to have a care of two things ; firft, that villanies be not encouraged with the rewards of virtue, which they will be, if the loweft and moft profligate characters, by dint of violence and of numbers, obtain the power of the ftate ; fecondly, that the authority and majefty of the government of this great nation be not defiled and expofed to public contempt, by the intrufion of men into

it

it who are objects of public averfion, as they would be of public juftice, if our laws poffeffed even the fmalleft portion of that feverity with which they have been fo unwarrantably reproached.

Having faid fufficient on the fubject of what thefe reformers call an *abufe*, I will not take notice of their infolence in pretending to *inftruct* us in the doctrine of *equal rights*, which they have lately broached, and would willingly eftablifh, until they have pulled down monarchy, and reduced the Throne and Nobility to a level with themfelves, the better to ufurp the power of the one and the property of the other, and then the enigma of equal rights will be woefully explained to us. Their meaning, indeed, is pretty evident, from their rags and ragged fortunes, but much more fo from their diffolute manners and morals. We are no longer uninformed that thefe rights mean

no

no right at all, although they would perfuade us that our advantage is the only
object they have in view. This promife,
fo delufive in the hope, and fo ruinous in
the event, refembles the compofitions of
apothecaries, who are ufed to mix fomething of relifh, fomething grateful to the
tafte, to qualify their bitter drugs, which
would otherwife be fpit out, and never
fwallowed.

That fuch doctrines fhould be publicly
recommended and maintained, is very af-
tonifhing; and ftill more fo, that the authors and promulgators of them fhould not
be punifhed ; for if this licence is to be allowed, and the public is to be difturbed
by the fenfelefs dreams, or difcontented
clamours of wild or factious men, it would
be much better that we return again to a
ftate of nature, where, at leaft, we would
be certain of having *one* right fecured to
us—*the right of the ftrongeft.* It has ever
been

been the firft and principal object of mankind, in all well-regulated governments, to preferve the public tranquillity, as on that alone depends the prefervation of life and property; and while they admit a fair and decent difcuffion of the general interefts of the community, to prohibit, under the fevereft penalties, whatever is likely to bring them into hazard. Indeed the very terms, *fociety and government*, imply certain rules and obligations incumbent upon thofe to obferve and obey who are benefited and protected by them; and without this obfervance and fubmiffion on their part, the laws would be without energy and effect, and the magiftrate without authority. The lives and fortunes of individuals would be in conftant jeopardy, and mutual confidence would no longer exift. No man in his fober fenfes, I am fure, would covet to live in a fociety where

where every thing, except mifchief and ruin, is fluctuating and uncertain, and where no one purpofe for which men affociate together is anfwered. There is nothing very pleafing in fuch a profpect; nothing feductive in fuch conditions; and yet it is precifely to this dangerous and precarious ftate, and that with an accumulating velocity, that the doctrine of EQUAL RIGHTS directly tends. If all men were equally wife and good, their purity and fagacity would fuperfede the neceffity of laws; their difcernment would lead them to felect, and their rectitude to prefer and adopt, whatever was prudent or juft; to avoid that which was wrong or improper: but the misfortune is, that all men are not equally fenfible and honeft, and while nature marks their minds and hearts with fuch ftrong and ftriking inequalities, thefe diftinctions will alfo continue to mark the different focieties into which mankind, for their

E   indi-

individual fafety, are compelled to enter.
Deftroy thefe wholefome, thefe neceffary
diftinctions in civil life, and *idlenefs* will
lord it over induftry; the *blockhead* will
out-top the man of fenfe; and the *knave*
fupplant the man of honour:—a very
Babel of confufion will enfue, and the
diftracted community become a prey to
Calibans and Trinculos without end.
Let this rabble of politicians and legiflators, iffuing forth like fo many dæmons
from their infernal abodes, with the bafe
coinage of their wicked and diftempered
brains in their mouths, fay what they will
to the contrary, there ever have been, and
ever will be, in all human focieties, *beadles*
for vagabonds, and *hangmen* for rogues and
affaffins. While fome men are lazy, and
fome are profligate, it will be neceffary
to force the one to work, and the other
to keep within bounds; hence the origin
of *punifhments:* and recompenfe being
certainly due to thofe, who by their genius,

nius, their bravery, or their fidelity, ferve the commonwealth, no one will deny the equity and utility of *rewards :* from hence proceed the diftinctions fo much complained of by thefe apoftles for what is called reformation, but which, in fact, means licence; for on whom, my Lord, are thofe titles and diftinctions beftowed, but on thofe who fight our battles on fea or on fhore, who defend our property from chicane, or who watch over our civil and religious liberties ? in a word, on our Admirals and Generals, our Judges and Statefmen ?

This fyftem of *equality* lately preached among us is certainly intended to injure thofe who have *nothing* to gain, and to benefit thofe who have *nothing* to lofe : from whence it is evident, that it is not fo much the *titles* of the Nobility and Gentry, as the well-earned fruits of their

talents,

talents; their integrity, and honourable
fcars, that they covet. They may be
envious of the fame and merit of our
Warriors and Legiflators, but it is the reward of that merit which they wifh to
feize; and the only way by which they
can hope to feize it, is to cry down the
King, Lords, and Commons, and force
themfelves into notice and authority in
their room. Such are the defigns of the
men whom your Lordfhip affects to
patronife, and whofe patronage you
would be compelled to court in your
turn fhould they carry their point—fuch
the pretenfions, my Lord, that we are
called upon to refift; and though we may
not be able to teach them better manners,
though we may find it difficult to fhame
them into filence, and though knaves
fometimes get into power by force, and
fools by chance; an univerfal choice and
election

election of knaves and fools for Government was never yet made by any who were not themfelves like thofe they chofe.

Thefe doctrines, maintained with a vehemence and effrontery to which we were ftrangers until the epoch of the French Revolution, are not the natural growth and produce of this temperate foil, but that of France, where it has become the fafhion, of late, to think every man equally qualified for the arduous offices of ftate, and where all men are become Kings, Minifters, Judges, Admirals, Generals, Bifhops, and Statefmen. This arrangement is held to be perfectly conformable to the unalienable rights of man, and as fuch, recommended to our example.

I am provoked to find that the more an event, calamitous in itfelf, and fatal to millions is reprobated by all honeft

and

and fenfible men, the more it is recommended by the weak and profligate
among us—as if poverty was preferable to
affluence; a tempeft to a calm; rifque to
fecurity; and anarchy to order! The
effrontery with which the French Revolution is conftantly held up to us for admiration, feems to augment in proportion to the contempt with which it is
treated. The partifans of the new Government in France (if a ftate of conftant
tumult and uproar, productive of mifchief, bloodfhed, and ruin, can be called
a Government) infift that we fhould imitate the example of our neighbours.—
They ftill contend that the National Convention in France fhould legiflate not only
for themfelves but for others—that this
piebald mixture of coblers, taylors, cooks,
barbers, and attornies, are the only men
of fcience; the only legiflators capable
of directing the affairs of this lower
world;

world; alone worthy to govern mankind; and that *wisdom* and *equity* are to be found no where but in their decrees. Wisdom and equity are high-founding words, and generally the loudest in the mouths of those, my Lord, who have the least share of either; but high-founding as they are, they certainly have a meaning, and that meaning is as obvious to us, and certainly as much within the scope of our capacities, as it is within the comprehension of those who pretend to judge what is best for us. I believe, my Lord, that the sense which I have affixed to these words, corresponds exactly with that which is given to them by the first men in point of rank, and no less so in point of abilities, that this country ever produced; of men, my Lord, whose names will ever be dear to their country, while honour and splendid talents have any hold on its affections. In the name

5

of

of Heaven, my Lord, for the appeal fhould
be awful and folemn that relates to the
prefent and future happinefs of mankind,
what infatuation, what phrenfy is this,
that ftimulates you to qualify as improvements what has proved fatal to millions?
What madnefs, imbecillity, or profligacy
muft have feized a mind, formed for better purpofes and fitted to better purfuits,
that ferioufly gives to the fouleft crimes
and moft extended mifchiefs, the virtues
and dignified appellations of wifdom and
of juftice! Turn your eyes, my Lord,
from that auguft, that venerable affembly, in which the valour of your anceftors gave you the right to deliberate—
from that dignified body, whofe authority your conduct has a tendency to degrade and annihilate—and behold without horror and indignation, if you can,
the terrible effects of that wifdom and of
that juftice which your Lordfhip would

feduce

feduce us to imitate. Let us examine to
what extremes of violence and abfurdity
this novel doctrine of equal rights may
be carried. Let us examine, my Lord, if
in the unqualified acceptation which has
been given to it by the French Convention, it differs from the wild and ferocious
fury of tigers. In order to bring the fubject more fully before you, and more im-
mediately home to your feelings and perfon, let us fuppofe that the enemies of the
Britifh Conftitution had fucceeded in obtaining a National Affembly in this country, fimilar to the one which wrefted the
fceptre from the imperfect grafp of Louis
the Sixteenth, and from the laws their
entire force, fplendour, and dignity. Let
us imagine, my Lord, for a moment (and
pray Heaven the fiction may never be re-
alifed!) that Great Britain is precifely in
the fame fituation as France was in 1790,
and that an impartial perfon with a cou-

F rage

rage proportioned to his zeal, knowledge,
and patriotifm, afcended the tribune, refolved at all events to expofe to his deluded countrymen the deplorable condition to which they were reduced.

In all probability his difcourfe would be
as follows; and I truft it will not be the lefs
acceptable to your Lordfhip for its being
a literal tranflation of a pathetic remon-
ftrance of the haplefs Clermont de Ton-
nere, who, like many others, was dragged
under and torn to pieces by the wheel,
which having fet in motion they had
neither the courage nor dexterity to ftop.

" There is no faying to what violence,
" abfurdity, and injuftice this novel doc-
" trine of equal rights may be extended.
" Let us ftrip it of its fafcinating and de-
" lufive drefs, let us analyfe this ftrange
" creed, which it is impoffible to compre-
" hend, and no lefs fo to practife, and fee
" to what it is reduced, when naked and
" deprived

" deprived of that fine and infectious tin-
" fel which has dazzled your fight and
" corrupted your minds.

" The doctrine, in fact, reduces itfelf
" to this—I am a man—confequently, I
" am free ; no man is or can be my fupe-
" rior; this world was created for me,
" and not being accountable to any one
" for my actions, I will do what I pleafe:
" having neither fortune nor induftry, I
" addrefs myfelf to the firft rich man that
" I meet, and demand the half of his pro-
" perty; he has the temerity to refufe
" me—I prefent the decree of the Na-
" tional Affembly with one hand, and a
" piftol with the other—demonftrate to
" him, that the Legiflature whom he
" fupports, and whom he is bound by
" oath to obey, has decided, that the no-
" bility and gentry have no longer any
" patrimony; that the rights they pof-
" feffed, by inheritance or purchafe, are

" tranf-

" transferred to the nation, of which I
" form a part, and that I claim nothing
" but what is abfolutely and juftly my
" due. Having no lodging, I fix myfelf
" in the firft convenient manfion that
" fuits me, and if my neighbour has a
" pretty wife or daughter, I will poffefs
" myfelf of one or the other, or both, if
" I like it. There is nothing more rea-
" fonable, according to the rights we have
" recently difcovered and obtained.——
" Such, my countrymen and fellow-citi-
" zens, or rather my fellow-fufferers, is
" the language that is held in the Pro-
" vinces—fuch the practice at prefent in
" vogue, and fuch the ftrange interpret-
" ation that has been given to the doc-
" trines lately broached amongft us—of
" the rights of man! Such is the abo-
" minable perverfion!—fuch the abufes
" that have already been committed, un-
" der the pretext of equality; and Heaven
" alone

" alone can tell where the miferies alrea-
" dy commenced will terminate !

" In the name of wonder, from whence
" comes this blind and unaccountable
" fubmiffion to the decrees of an Affem-
" bly, compofed of all that is vile and illi-
" terate ? They have ufurped the fove-
" reign authority, and they hold you in
" a ftate of vaffalage, more dreadful, and
" infinitely more difgraceful, than what
" you or your anceftors ever experienced
" under the ancient form of government.
" You do not believe that you are flaves,
" becaufe you have been told that you
" are free. Your ears have been tickled
" with high-founding words, and their
" teftimony is to contradict the evidence
" of your fenfes ! You are goaded, and
" you do not feel ; you are laughed at,
" and will not perceive it ; you are on the
" edge of a precipice, and will neither fee
" nor avoid the gulph below you !—

" Open

" Open your eyes and tremble at the hor-
" rors that furround you ! Behold reli-
" gion degraded from her fublime and
" confolatory functions ; her minifters
" perfecuted and plundered ; your nobi-
" lity beggared and banifhed ; your be-
" loved fovereign a clofe prifoner ; his
" life menaced, and his haplefs, helplefs
" infants advancing, not to fplendour
" and independence, but to forrow, mi-
" fery, and difgrace, and that with more
" rapidity than they advance to matu-
" rity ! Do you think the picture over-
" charged—or that the diftrefs I have de-
" fcribed is confined folely to the King
" and his family ? No ! it has pervaded
" the entire nation ; the calamity is ge-
" neral, and the country is ruined ! You
" have neither trade nor commerce to
" animate induftry, or feed the millions
" that lived by the fweat of their brow !
" Your artificers, thrown out of employ-
" ment,

" ment, infeft your ftreets as mendicants,
" or your highways as robbers! The
" revenue, materially injured by the ge-
" neral ftagnation of traffic, bears no pro-
" portion to an heavy and increafed ex-
" penditure! The fraudulent expedient
" of paper-money, called in aid to the
" alarming deficiency, cannot anfwer the
" current expences of the nation ; and as
" its value is decreafing daily in the pub-
" lic opinion, its depreffion, and the total
" extinction of public credit, muft accele-
" rate the bankruptcy we have fo long
" expected. Look to the adminiftration
" of the kingdom, if it can be fo called
" without an abufe of the word, and you
" will difcover nothing but univerfal
" gloom, diftruft, and confufion! nothing
" confpicuous but defpondency, and the
" wide-extended mifchiefs that defolate
" the country, from the Pyrenees to the
" Rhine! Look to the police of Paris,

2   " fo

" fo much admired by all Europe, before
" the Revolution, and compare its former
" ftate with what it is at prefent! The
" beft regulated city in the world is
" become a receptacle for vagabonds,
" thieves, and affaffins, who commit
" their depredations in the broad glare
" of day, in defiance of the THING
" whom you have decorated with the
" title of Mayor, and of your Comman-
" der in Chief.—In the former, we be-
" hold a magiftrate without refpect; in
" the latter, a general without authority;
" and to fuch *beings* (God help us!) is
" the fafety of this vaft metropolis, and
" indeed of the whole nation, confided!
" You fay that you are no longer flaves;
" if fo, from whence proceeds that refpect
" for thofe numerous Committees of Se-
" cret Inquiry more arbitrary in their
" execution, and more terrible in their ef-
" fects, than the moft confirmed defpo-
" tifm?

" tifm ? What is the real intent of thofe
" dark Committees ? Surely you need not
" be told, that it is to extinguifh the
" poor remains you yet poffefs of honour
" and humanity, to eradicate, in your
" minds, every fentiment of dignity and
" virtue, and to familiarize you with
" fcenes of blood, by rendering you af-
" faffins and informers !

" You are not flaves, and why ? Be-
" caufe you have dethroned your King,
" whofe fole ftudy it has been to render
" you happy, and whofe reward, for all
" the paternal kindnefs he has fhewn
" you, may be death—the murder of his
" young and unoffending offspring, and the
" extinction of his name and family !—
" The other proofs you have given of your
" freedom, are no lefs glorious—you have
" attempted to affaffinate the Queen ; and
" you again menace her, that if the Em-
" peror, as chief of the Empire, fhould be

" obliged

" obliged to fupport the claims of the
" Princes whom you have plundered,
" that you will difplay her bleeding head,
" fevered from her mangled fhoulders, on
" a pole! Houfes have been pillaged and
" burnt; their unoffending inhabitants
" driven into exile or wantonly maffacred,
" and all the legal reftraints removed from
" men, whofe depravity of minds, more
" than their defperate fortunes, urge
" them to riot, robbery, and murder!

" Juft heavens! What a world of mif-
" chief has a few months produced! and
" to complete this fad eventful hiftory,
" the empire of a great nation, of a nation
" that has made Europe tremble—anni-
" hilated for ever! If it is yet poffible
" to awaken you from your infatuation,
" open your eyes, and behold your de-
" plorable condition! Are you happier
" than you were before the Revolution?
" Surely not—for you confefs that you
" are

" are ftarving; that your trade is ruined,
" and that you have no employment.
" In what then confifts this boafted
" regeneration of the State? In what
" confifts the fuperlative virtue of the
" new fyftem, when it neither gives
" employment to the induftrious, pro-
" tection to the weak, nor fecurity to the
" affluent? You muft acknowledge that
" the National Affembly has never ftu-
" died your interefts in any one of the De-
" crees that it has paffed, nor meant
" to relieve your grievances; on the
" contrary, it is evident, by the Decree
" againft the Nobility, that they would
" drive you to defpair. As this Decree
" (which is meant to diffolve all ranks and
" diftinctions, but which it never can
" accomplifh) affects you more particu-
" larly than any other, it may not be
" improper to inquire what advantage
" the people can acquire, when there are
" no longer any Barons and Counts,

G 2   " Dukes

" Dukes and Marquifes, and Princes of
" the Blood. The peafant—will he be
" lefs a peafant when there are no more
" Lords? The cobler—will he not remain
" fo, though nobility fhould be deftroyed?
" will he be elevated becaufe the other is
" degraded? will he become richer, or
" will he live more comfortably? You
" are convinced to the contrary. What
" then do you gain by this abfurd and ex-
" travagant law? Nothing. Then I will
" tell you what you lofe by it—twenty
" thoufand workmen, at leaft, are impo-
" verifhed and reduced to beggary, whofe
" bufinefs it was to fabricate livery-cloths
" and laces; and not only thefe manufac-
" turers are injured by this Decree, but the
" merchants who import the raw mate-
" rials, the fhopkeeper who vends them
" when manufactured; and, furely, it
" needs no great pains to convince you,
" that if you perfecute the clafs in fociety
" that confumes the moft, your trade
" will

" will be ruined, and your town rendered
" a defert. The riches and opulence of
" this great town was occafioned by the
" great concourfe with which it abounded
" of nobility and men of confiderable
" property : its vicinity to the moft bril-
" liant Court in Europe, and its being
" the refort of innumerable ftrangers of
" the firft diftinction, who fpent the
" greateft part of their incomes amongft
" you. If you deprive your own nobility
" of the means of obtaining the luxuries
" furnifhed by yourfelves, the inferior
" orders of fociety, which always imitate
" the great, will, of courfe, be obliged to
" relinquifh them alfo, and foreigners of
" rank will, certainly, no longer frequent
" a country, where rank is regarded with
" horror, and treated with rigour. All this
" influx of money, this fource of wealth
" to the nation, will be deftroyed, and
" your metropolis forfaken by the nobi-
" lity,

" lity, and people of fortune will ne-
" ceffarily be deferted by thofe who de-
" pended on them for fupport. This it
" well behoves you to reflect upon; but
" is there even one decree by which you
" can fay that you are fubftantially be-
" nefited? What is become of the im-
" menfe property which has been confif-
" cated from its ancient and legal pro-
" prietors, under the infamous pretext of
" converting it to *your* ufe? You have
" been told, that you have no longer any
" duties to difcharge, or rents to pay to
" your landlords. This is the firft in-
" ftance, upon record, of a Legiflature
" committing a public and deliberate
" theft on the property of thoufands;
" but atrocious and horrible as the act
" in itfelf is, the confequences refulting
" from it are ftill more fo : it has excited
" you to robbery and revolt, without
" permitting you to derive any thing

4   " from

" from your crimes, but the infamy be-
" longing to them. You have beggared
" the proprietors of land, and your for-
" tunes are not mended; on the con-
" trary, they are worfe! The duties you
" formerly paid were fo trifling, that they
" were fcarce perceptible; for the half-
" crown that you annually paid, you
" received an hundred. The payment of
" this trifle could be no object to you in-
" dividually, but taken collectively, it
" was a very great one to your landlord :
" it was his fubfiftence ; it enabled him to
" employ you, to adminifter relief to you
" in the moment of diftrefs, and to aid
" your helplefs families. Deprived of
" the means, he can no longer fly to
" your fuccour, even if he had the in-
" clination, and could forget your ingra-
" titude !

   " Agriculture is fufpended by his ab-
" fence; the cheerful farm is become a
                     " mi-

" miferable defert; the fields no longer
" bear a rich and luxuriant crop ; and far
" from being benefited by the exemption,
" much heavier taxes than ever are laid
" on you, and augmented in proportion as
" your ability to pay them decreafes! You
" rejoice in your exemption from tithes, but
" you forget that the tax impofed upon
" you in their ftead, is far more oppreffive.
" Let the harveft, in future, be good or
" bad, you muft pay the fame; whereas,
" formerly, if the feafon proved unkind,
" the prieft had nothing to receive; you
" were not accountable for the caprice
" of the weather, and were only held to
" pay in proportion as it was favourable,
" and the foil you cultivated was grate-
" ful.

" The change has placed you in a
" worfe fituation than it found you.
" The inundation that drowns the rich
" crop; the torrent that wafhes it away;
" the

" the blight that deftroys, and the tem-
" peft that fweeps it to a level with the
" earth, are of no avail : the rector and
" vicar muft be paid, and you not only
" lofe the produce of your labour, but
" you are now obliged to advance money
" out of your pockets !

" You have been told, that the Ga-
" belle is fuppreffed, and fo it ought to
" be; I was the firft to propofe it : but
" is this folitary and partial benefit to
" compenfate for all the evils you endure,
" or to atone for your paying one hun-
" dred and twenty millions (1,250,000l.
" fterling) in lieu of the fixty to which
" the old tax upon falt amounted? Thefe
" calculations are not beyond your capa-
" city, if you will give yourfelves the trou-
" ble to reflect. And when you come to
" ftrike a balance of debtor and creditor,
" and compare what you have LOST with
" what you have *gained*, Lord have

H   " mercy

" mercy upon thofe who have deceived
" you!

" In order to dazzle your eyes, as well
" as your underftandings, you have been
" treated (that is, at your own expence)
" with what your *honeft* mafters are
" pleafed to call a Confederation.

" The enthufiafm, or rather the de-
" lirium of the moment (and pray Hea-
" ven it may only be the delirium of
" a moment!) is certainly favourable
" to their purpofe: not content with
" putting you to the daily and enor-
" mous expence of 24,000 livres (1050l.
" fterling) for their daily fupport, they
" have made preparations to celebrate the
" deftruction of their country, fo im-
" menfe and fo expenfive, that they would
" have alarmed even the oftentatious
" and unfeeling prodigality of Louis the
" XIVth.

" But what is expence; what are the
" mines

" mines of Peru and Mexico, compared
" to the capture of the Baftile! the
" governor of which loft his head
" long before you took it off his fhoul-
" ders, or you would never have ta-
" ken it; and who having neither
" troops, ammunition, nor provifion,
" might be expected to furrender the in-
" ftant he was attacked. Great proof of
" magnanimity, truly, to difarm a dozen
" old men with rufty firelocks, without
" powder or ball! Yet this is the heroic
" feat, for which fuch vaft preparations
" were made, and which you have the
" vanity to fuppofe that other nations
" will celebrate, with the fame degree of
" folly that you have done! But for what
" purpofe is all this parade? Is it to re-
" joice at the demolition of an old for-
" trefs, which was formidable only to
" thofe whom you now trample under
" foot? for the nobility alone were con-

H 2   " fined

" fined in it, and had the moft reafon to
" complain of it.   The *Bicêtre*, and other
" common jails, were allotted for your re-
" ception, and they exift ftill : there you
" are ftill confined, and they are more
" crowded than ever.   Hence *confinement*,
" you fee, is not abolifhed in this land of
" *freedom!* on the contrary, your fellow-
" citizens are piled one upon another,
" three deep, in thefe loathfome dun-
" geons, not charged with any fpecific
" crime, but merely fufpected of the fin
" of ariftocracy—that is, of preferring or-
" der to anarchy—they have been im-
" mured for months, feparated from the
" world, and prohibited all correfpond-
" ence with their friends and relations,
" without the leaft profpect of their being
" brought to a fair and equitable trial;
" yet this, in the new vocabulary of the
" Jacobins, is called Liberty.

  " That the tumult may be as great as
                                    " poffible,

" poffible, and diforder perpetuated, the
" whole nation was invited to affift at this
" grand Confederation.

" Proftitute fcribblers, without talents
" or principle, affure you, that neither
" Athens nor Rome ever produced any
" thing half fo magnificent. Not that
" you know much of the matter, or wifh
" to know; you believe it, and that's
" enough. But for what purpofe are you
" affembled? Is it to fwear fidelity to the
" King? You have already done it. Is
" it to fwear fidelity to the Conftitution?
" Where is it? Prove to me that fuch a
" thing really exifts in France, and what-
" ever form or fhape it may have, I will
" fwear to maintain it at the hazard of
" my life and fortune; my oath, degraded
" as the clafs is to which I belong, is yet
" of fome value, and will have fome
" weight in the country.

" Deluded, cozened fools! you have
" no

" no Conſtitution ! But you ſay that
" you are to have one—that is, you have
" been told ſo—and that it cannot be
" otherwiſe, becauſe the King has given
" his ſanction. And are you really ſo ea-
" ſily deceived ? Are you really ſo blind
" or ſo ſtupid as not to ſee that your King
" is no longer a King ? that, deſcending
" voluntarily from his throne to receive
" and redreſs your complaints, he was
" dragged, by the rude hand of ruffian
" violence, to the bottom, and ſtripped
" at once of his crown and ſceptre : the
" mantle of royalty has been torn from
" his ſhoulders, and even the very ſha-
" dow of authority taken from him !

" Do not you perceive that he is more
" a ſlave than any of you ? that his
" ſanction and nothing mean the ſame
" thing ; and that if a decree, prohibiting
" thoſe who have breeches to wear them,
" ſhould be preſented to him for accept-

3   " ance,

" ance, he would be compelled to give it
" his sanction, as he was to the test oath
" prescribed for the clergy, on the 27th
" of last November, and which would
" have rested neglected and contemned,
" without effect, but for the potent and
" auxiliary aid of the mob? What merit,
" what virtue can there be in a sanction,
" where a negative is denied?—Has the
" King a right to refuse? You know
" that he has not. What an insult
" then to common sense to talk of
" the Royal Assent! In the same man-
" ner, taxes upon taxes are imposed
" to the full amount of thirty-six per
" cent. on your incomes, more than
" what you paid under the ancient sys-
" tem; yet enormous and oppressive as
" they are, you cannot refuse to pay them
" without being guilty of perjury. But
" could you get over this obstacle, and
" which may not be very difficult, con-
                              " sidering

" fidering the torrent of irreligion and im-
" morality with which we are inundated,
" how will you be able to get clear of the
" foldiery ?   They have fworn to enforce
" obedience to the decrees of the National
" Affembly, and the bayonet, you well
" know, is an effectual remedy for a flex-
" ible confcience.   You muft not ima-
" gine that the military will perjure
" themfelves a *fecond* time to indulge your
" convenience or caprice, unlefs, indeed,
" you can add ten fols (five-pence) a day
" to their pay, and fecure it to them for
" ever.   In this manner, you all know,
" they were firft debauched ; and do you
" think that the National Affembly (as
" it calls itfelf) will permit you to turn
" the tables upon them by a fimilar ma-
" nœuvre ?   If you do, you have lefs
" fenfe than I thought you had.   But
" left the army and militia fhould not
" be difpofed to go all lengths with your
                                    " prefent

" prefent tyrants, the mob has been en-
" lifted into their fervice. By this annual
" facrifice of forty-five millions of the
" public revenue (two millions fterling*)
" wine and brandy, in Paris, have been
" purpofely lowered in price, while bread,
" meat, and all the neceffaries of life, are
" dearer than ever. For what purpofe
" is this difference, but to keep the bulk
" of the people in a conftant ftate of in-
" toxication, left, in a lucid interval of
" reafon, they fhould become fenfible of
" their melancholy fituation, and take
" ample vengeance on the authors of
" their misfortunes? It is not very eafy

---

* This is rather underftated, for Mr. Necker efti-
mates les droits d'entrée at full forty-eight millions of
French livres, and this calculation will not appear ex-
travagant, when it is confidered that every article, without exception, paid a duty on entering Paris : wine,
for example, paid near five fols each bottle (full two-
pence halfpenny Englifh).

" to

" to guefs by what means this confider-
" able lofs of revenue will be fupplied;
" the duties paid on entering of the town
" were too important to have been idly
" relinquifhed, and efpecially as the be-
" nefits refulting from their abolition can
" be no object. In addition to the lofs
" fuftained, the State muft make a fuit-
" able provifion for thofe who were em-
" ployed to collect thofe duties, and hence
" new taxes become neceffary. The
" church has no more lands to lofe and
" nothing to give. The nobility, indeed,
" have yet fomething left, and the foli-
" tary million of livres (43,656 l. 5s. fter-
" ling) to which you have cut down the
" Princes of the Blood, may yet, perhaps,
" be thought too much, and be reduced
" to half that fum. But even thefe de-
" predations and retrenchments will not
" produce forty-five millions of livres.
" And, furely, it is worthy of your atten-
" tion

" tion to inquire how this deficiency is to
" be made good, and whether the de-
" ftruction of the barriers was not a com-
" pliment to the rabble of Paris, to fecure
" their good-humour, and, in cafe of ne-
" ceffity, their fupport. Such is the true
" ftate of your affairs, and yet you deem
" thofe acts lawful and juft! The fober
" part of mankind, believe me, think very
" different; they confider them as ufurpa-
" tions and oppreffions! and fo will you,
" when the film is removed that obfcures
" your fight. Now behold the fum to-
" tal of your calamities, and blufh at the
" infamy you have entailed upon your
" name and country for ages!

" Behold your King a captive, and his
" life in danger! Your Queen, whofe fex
" alone entitles her to refpect, daily in-
" fulted, and holding her exiftence at the
" mercy of a ferocious and fanguinary
" rabble!

" The

" The innocent offspring of your So-
" vereign witnefs to the unmerited per-
" fecutions of their unhappy father, par-
" taking of ·his misfortunes whilft he
" lives, and doomed to inherit them
" when he is dead !

" Your courts of juftice abolifhed, and
" claims of property to an enormous
" amount left undecided.

" The arbitrary will of a licentious
" mob, or the more methodical defpo-
" tifm of the army, fupplying the place
" of law !

" The Metropolis in conftant riot and
" alarm !

" The Provinces deluged in blood by
" civil commotion !

" Your Colonies in rebellion to your
" authority, and at war amongft them-
" felves !

" Your manufactures languifhing—
" Your commerce almoft annihilated—
" No

" No money in the country, and the
" paper of little value—

" Your fellow-citizens, of rank and
" fortune, driven into exile, and the mil-
" lions who lived by their fplendour, be-
" come a ponderous and dangerous bur-
" then to the State—

" Sons fighting againft their fathers,
" and brothers againft brothers; every
" man armed fufpicious of an enemy in
" his neighbour; and the whole nation,
" as it were, in open hoftility againft itfelf
" and all the world!

" Thefe are facts, melancholy exifting
" facts, the effects of which you will woe-
" fully feel, whenever you recover from
" your prefent delirium.

" Can you reconcile them with the
" principles on which Society exifts,
" or on which any Government what-
" ever can be fupported? You know
" that you cannot. What honeft and

8   " fenfible

" fenfible man then, but muft wifh in
" his heart, that the authority awarded to
" the King fhould be confirmed, and the
" laws refpected—without which the
" horrors of anarchy will augment daily,
" the infamous authors of the public dif-
" trefs, in order to attach the ragged,
" the indigent, and profligate to their
" caufe, will, when they can no longer
" bribe them with money or affignats,
" ftimulate them to pillage your houfes,
" divide your eftates, and the maffacre of
" your army will follow the plunder of
" your fortunes."

Such was the pathetic difcourfe of a
man whofe benevolence of heart and purity of mind could not fhield him from the
malevolence of fufpicion. He was among
the firft who fell a victim to the intrigues
and cabals of men who had made him
the inftrument of their criminal ambition.
Believe me, my Lord, this melancholy
detail

detail of the calamities of his unhappy country is not exaggerated. Contrast then, I beseech you, the ruin he describes and felt, with the blessings which you contemplate and enjoy. Behold your country flourishing and free in commercial profitable intercourse with the four quarters of the habitable globe; happy at home and respected abroad! Behold the Thames cheerful, animated, and industrious, floating to the proud metropolis of Britain the rich tributes of the known world; while the Seine, pensive, disconsolate, and surcharged with blood, ebbs mournfully and dejected a crimson current to the sea! Reflect on the gloom and havoc which mark one country, and on the joy and prosperity diffused throughout the other. That other, my Lord, is your own; and as the wealth, grandeur, and felicity she displays are incontrovertible proofs of

the

the wisdom and equity of her Government, spurn I conjure you the vermin who would impress on your too facile mind a contrary opinion, in order to embark you in schemes of guilt and dishonour. Whichever way you direct your attention, you find affluence and content, freedom and happiness; and with such strong vouchers before you of comfort and security, can your Lordship question the prosperous condition of your country? If France felt herself enslaved (and who can doubt it?) she did well to break her fetters; but what chains, what bondage, have Englishmen to break, and what knowledge can they derive from their sanguinary neighbours, but the foul register of their crimes and misfortunes, the black and voluminous catalogue of unprovoked cruelties, proscriptions, and massacres? Yet under this terrible pressure fure of accumulated infamy we are told the French are wife and happy! My Lord, it is impoffible ; for guilt and happinefs are incompatible.

It is not denied that the abufe in the ancient Government of France called loudly for redrefs. It is univerfally acknowledged that thofe who had the management of the public intereft in that diftracted kingdom, had oppreffed the people by exorbitant taxes, and beggared the treafury by the moft fcandalous profufion and embezzlement. The vexations were certainly enormous, and the mifchiefs of an extent that required to be inftantly ftopped, but there was not virtue enough in the country to accomplifh the defired reform ; and when it was attempted, a number of factious difcontented people blazed forth, who bark at all abufes but thofe which they commit. Thefe difcontented people (fuch, my Lord, as are to

K   be

be found in all nations) obtained by clamour and intrigue admiffion into the legiflative affemblies, and abufing the innocent fimplicity of their countrymen, they
changed their tone; and wrefting from
the King, already a cypher in his dominions, the fmall remains of power he poffeffed, infifted that the right to reform
and eftablifh refted folely with them, and
that the duty of the fovereign was merely
to fanction what they decided.

The right to approve implies a right to condemn, and it would be hard indeed if thofe
who have the privilege to receive had not
alfo the liberty to reject. This appears to be
the foundation, the very bafis, as it were,
of all equity ; but the obligation to abfolutely receive, and pofitively to approve
of *every* thing, is a tyranny of a nature
more foul in its complection, and more
diabolical in its confequences, than any
that has been tranfmitted to us from ancient

cient times, and which certainly exceeds every example that modern hiftory can produce of oppreffion and vexation. Yet fuch is the tyranny which factious, feditious, and enterprifing men in France exercife at this inftant over their degraded countrymen, and which factious, feditious, and enterprifing men in our country, my Lord, would, if they could, introduce and eftablifh in this.

Such has been. the equity, the *juftice*, and *decency* of the French ; I beg your Lordfhip to examine what has been their WISDOM: they have deftroyed the old form of Government, becaufe it was bad, and they replaced it by a wild and remorfelefs defpotifm—the defpotifm of thoufands, who iffued from all the nighthoufes, gambling-houfes, brothels, and dunghills in France, the inftant the National Affembly reduced the King from being the firft man in point of power in

K 2   the

the nation, to be the laft! If the French really poffeffed this wonderful knowledge, this extraordinary fkill in the fcience of government, what excufe can be offered, or what good reafon can be given for their having left their country a prey to civil difcord for near four years? and what muft the world think of this boafted capacity, fo much cried up by defigning knaves in that country, and repeated like fo many echoes by their affociates, and the fenfelefs blockheads they have feduced in this, when it cannot ftop the mifchiefs, nor put an end to the confufion that reigns in every part of that ruined country?

Under the pretence of reforming the different departments in the ftate, they abolifhed them; and if abolition means reformation, no reformation I confefs was ever fo extenfive and complete, for there is not a veftige at this hour remaining of

any

any one eftablifhment, either civil, military, or ecclefiaftic, that exifted on the
14th of July 1789. The foldiery have
long fince rejected all difcipline; and as
to the church, it has been fo pared and
cut down, that the venerable edifice is no
longer known, even to themfelves. In
a word, there is no Government in
France, and where there is no Government, there can be no liberty; all order,
decency, and fubordination are at an end.
This is what the philofophy of the times
calls reducing things to their firft principles; that is, diffolving all the ties of
fociety, cancelling all obligations to God
from man, and between man and man,
in order to begin the world anew—Kings,
Magiftrates, Priefts, Soldiers, and all the
different fprings, checks, and fecurities of
focial life are diffolved into one common
mafs, and man reduced to his forlorn and
primitive condition, without fuccour, protection,

tection, or comfort of any kind—reduced to the favage ftate of his rude and uncultivated anceftors, immerfed in all the evils attendant on the vagrant and defencelefs lives they led in woods and deferts, without the plea of ignorance to excufe it, and without their purity and fimplicity to confole him; and this it is that the little knots of obfcure individuals, in different parts of this kingdom, affuming to themfelves the confequence of legalifed affemblies, and meeting in bye holes and corners, have the infolence to call WISDOM; while the plunder of eftates and of churches, the licence of general and indifcriminate robbery, outrage, and maffacre, are termed by thefe fame anonymous clubs of midnight legiflators, to be EQUITY. But what WISDOM is there in the conduct that voluntarily fpurns eafe, affluence, and fecurity, for difgraceful toil, poverty, and danger? And what rectitude

titude of mind muſt thoſe poſſeſs, my Lord, who aſſert in the face of Heaven and the world, that the violence that wreſts from its peaceable and legal poſ-feſſor, the honeſt produce of his induſtry, or the property he holds by hereditary deſcent, the reward, perhaps, of military or of civic virtue, is wiſe and EQUITABLE? The inſtant theſe doctrines became *le-galiſed* in France, they were practiſed, and the practice has extended from Paris to St. Domingo, and to all her diſtant poſ-feſſions in the Eaſt and in the Weſt. This new-diſcovered wiſdom has convert-ed the happineſs of the affluent planters into miſery; changed hope into deſpon-dency, and rendered even exiſtence itſelf painful, and almoſt diſhonourable.

The Negroes, adopting the EQUITABLE maxims of the great lawgivers in France, after having ſet fire to the plantations of their benevolent maſters; plundered their

bene-

benefactors, ravifhed and murdered their wives and daughters, are themfelves compelled to feek refuge in the receffes of fteep and difficult mountains; from whofe barren and inhofpitable fummits they contemplate in grief and defpondency the valleys in which they have fpread devaftation and ruin, and in which they revelled, when the fetting fun, releafing them from labour, difmiffed them to rural fports and paftimes. Ten thoufand of thefe haplefs wretches have perifhed the unlamented victims of their guilt and folly—fugarworks and eftates have been deftroyed, to the amount of as many millions fterling —the rich commercial towns of Bourdeaux, Marfeilles, Nantz, Havre, and Rouen, are reduced to a ftate of bankruptcy by the lofs of that commerce which fupported and enriched them. The planters are plunged from a ftate of fplendour to want even the common neceffaries of

life;

life; beggary is entailed on their helpless posterity; and an island, equal in extent almost to that of England, was in a state of anarchy and confusion, that rendered equally insecure both life and property, until it fell under the dominion of Britain.

Such have been the direful effects of this junction of WISDOM and EQUITY, as it is called, and which is so impudently recommended to our example by men in this country, rendered desperate by their poverty and their crimes, and who seem to have entered into a confederacy with men of a similar description in France, for the total subversion, not only of our happy constitution, but of all order and government in the known world. Among the sad variety of woe which appears destined to mark the close of the eighteenth century, is that of attempting to accomplish the entire dissolution of all religion among us. It is the misfortune of the present time to affect

L   a spirit

a fpirit of toleration, not out of compaf-
fion for error, not from any particular regard for this, or that, or any other fect,
but from an indifference bordering on
contempt for all fects and perfuafions.
This *pretended* toleration is nothing more,
in fact, than *concealed* atheifm; I do not
mean that placid and unaffuming atheifm
which is the refult of deep metaphyfical
refearch, of profound abftract reafoning,
which even the mind the moft virtuoufly
difpofed may, from not being able to pro-
cure the proofs neceffary to its own conviction, be led to *doubt*, and then to *deny*,
but that fpecies of atheifm which is the
refult of vice, and that is confirmed by
profligate habits : the former fpecies of
atheifm, the produce of *too much* or of *too
little* reflection, extends no farther than the
clofet, for it means no ill; but the other
has its fource in vicious propenfities, and
as it can only hope for impunity in the
extinction of *all* religion, it leaves no
meafures

meafures unattempted, by which its direful contagion may fpread itfelf over the furface of the earth. If you look to your friends, my Lord, in France, you will find the truth of this obfervation moft woefully confirmed, by the demolition of all the fences and all the barriers which morality and piety had erected for the fecurity of virtue : every beacon which exifted heretofore has been deftroyed, and the whole country exhibits a wild and fterile heath, affording neither hope nor confolation to the wayworn and bewildered traveller. This is the atheifm that is extending its baneful influence throughout the habitable world ; which fome men are wickedly endeavouring to introduce among us, and which means *guilt*, though it profeffes *innocence* ;—that practical and diabolical atheifm, the mifchievous and deformed offspring of depravity (not the mild and inoffenfive child of fpeculation);

that

that licence, that blafphemes all religions, and confounds all the diſtinctions of right; which is meant to fanction crimes and every fpecies of diforder. My Lord, there is fraud legibly written on every feature of this *baſtard* toleration. It means nothing lefs than the fubverfion of all ecclefiaftical eſtabliſhments, and to inundate the country with vice and profligacy of every defcription. Its object is to overwhelm the country with a torrent of irreligion and diffolute philofophy, intended to contract the heart to all fenfe of virtue, in proportion as it expands and adapts the mind to the reception of every fpecies of vice-and immorality. Independent of the blafphemy of fuch attempts; independent of the profligacy that produced them; and of the ſtill greater profligacy that would refult from them, if they fhould prove fuccefsful, there is fomething fo intolerably gloomy in fcepticifm;

ticifm; fomething in it fo directly tending
to defpair, that there is cruelty to mankind
as well as infult and ingratitude to the Di-
vinity, in endeavouring to flacken the
bonds that connect them with heaven and
eternity.

There is fomething fo exhilarating in
the very idea of religion, that, exclufive of
its folemnity, and the affurance it gives
of falvation and happinefs hereafter, I am
amazed that, on the fcore of mirth, and
of that cheerfulnefs which it never fails
to produce in the minds and hearts of
men, that any effort fhould be made,
or any wifh formed, to ftop up the fource
of fo much prefent comfort and delight,
and of fo much future hope and confolation. Surely, my Lord, there is no fubject
more proper for our ftudy and contem-
plation, or a queftion of greater moment,
than the one which to a certainty involves
in it not only our own immediate advantage

tage and profperity, but the general felicity of the whole human race; for, take
away the fubftantial prop of religion
from civil fociety, and what can preferve
it from anarchy and defolation? What
other fufficient fecurity has honeft induftry for the produce of its well-earned
labour? and what a ruthlefs and favage
wild will be opened to our view, if that
fecurity fhould be deftroyed or removed!
Take away the fublime and confolatory
aid of religion from man in his individual
capacity, and to what a ftate of wretched-
nefs and defpondency do you reduce him!
In either cafe, my Lord, the evils which
would refult from this dangerous and
levelling fyftem of confounding all religions, and diffolving them, as it were, into
one common mafs, from whence nothing
but guilt, mifery, and defpair can arife,
are beyond all eftimate. Figure to yourfelf the Laws deprived of their *force*; the
Magi-

Magiſtrates of their *authority*; Man of his laſt and deareſt *hope*; and Providence of that adoration which is due from our inferiority to its wiſdom, and from our gratitude to its goodneſs; and your Lordſhip will then have a tolerable idea of the ſtate and condition to which thoſe modern apoſtles for liberty of conſcience would reduce us.

Nothing can be of greater import to ſociety, my Lord, than the preſervation of order. Without it, this world would be a ſavage, ſterile wild, full of difficulties and of danger, affording neither peace nor comfort to its miſerable and diſperſed inhabitants; and yet, my Lord, it is this very order, ſo neceſſary to our felicity and ſupport, that ſweetens exiſtence and confirms our happineſs, that your Lordſhip is labouring as effectually to deſtroy, as if its deſtruction had become the favourite object of your purſuits. It can be no

ſecret.

fecret (for they have voted you public
thanks, and they occafionally correfpond
with your Lordfhip), that there are a fet
of men in this country who feek to fubvert the elegant, compact, and well-tem-
pered production of Britifh wifdom and
heroifm; who arrogating to themfelves
the power and capacity which belong to
none of us individually, but to all of us
collectively, would reduce us to the infig-
nificance of cyphers, or whatever elfe in
their profound wifdom they would pleafe
to make of us.

For my part, I have ever confidered
the Britifh Conftitution as an hiftorical
painting of prodigious beauty and magnitude, executed by the moft eminent mafters, in which the progrefs of civilization
from the date of Magna Charta to that of
the Bill of Rights may be feen at one view;
nor does it require any extraordinary
effort of the imagination to perfonify
and

and reprefent to itfelf this vaft and wonderful affemblage of laws, manners, and cuf-
toms, on which the whole fabric of fociety
has been conftructed and happily brought
to perfection. The mind, my Lord, dwells
with pleafure on the fictions it creates, while
reafon, an accomplice in the cheat, fhapes
them into form, and deceives the judgment
into a belief of their exiftence. The fublime and interefting picture above mentioned is conftantly before me. I ftudy it
with attention, and gaze in rapture on the
glorious achievements of our heroic ancef-
ftors. I behold them in the very dawn
and infancy of reafon, before the mild
but irrefiftible influence of manners pre-
vailed, *repelling* Defpotifm, and *reftraining*
Anarchy, until, from a chaos of rude and
difcordant materials, a rational and well
harmonized fyftem of Government arofe,
the pride and wonder of mankind, of
which the King, Lords and Commons

M   were

were declared to be the *perpetual* and *hereditary* Guardians. To them alone are confided our civil and religious liberties; they hold them in truſt for *us* and our *heirs* for ever; and where can we find truſtees of more wiſdom and integrity, or of equal reſponſibility? And would your Lordſhip join the ſhameleſs and nameleſs herd of beings, who, confederated in guilt, are diſperſed throughout the kingdom to deface, and finally deſtroy this ſublime and beautiful, this hiſtorical and at once inſtructive and amuſing picture, the immenſe and perilous labour of ages! the admiration of ſucceſſive generations, and the beſt legacy we can bequeath to poſterity? I cannot, dare not, my Lord, think ſo ill of you! Induſtrious however and zealous as theſe Revolution-mongers and Government-makers may be, in a buſineſs of ſuch foul and infernal import, I truſt they will be

dif.

difappointed, and that the Britifh Conftitution, fuperior to the rude affaults of its
profligate enemies, will even triumph over
the ravages of time, and continue to be
the fence and rampart of religion and
virtue, as it has ever been that of learning
and of freedom, until it falls in the general wreck and diffolution of the world.
My Lord, this bold and audacious attack was carried on under reftraint and
awe, and even with occafional fymp-
toms of remorfe for the atrocity of the
attempt, until the officious and intemperate
perate zeal of a man *, who is always in
the

---

* The cowardly attack made on an unfortunate individual immured in a dungeon, and unable to defend himfelf from the flanders which have been advanced with a
degree of impudence proportioned to their turpitude and
falfehood, provoked me to vindicate his character from
the illiberal afperfions of his malevolent and unfeeling
adverfary. I have oppofed facts to affertions, and left
the world to decide on the brutal infolence of a man
raifed into confequence more by favour than by merit;

and

the extremes, and whofe whole life is little
elfe than a feries of contradiction, abfur-
dities

and whofe life exhibits, in ftrong colours, a tiffue of all
the meanneffes which degrade our common nature.—It
is proved in a publication which I have avowed, though
my name is not affixed to it, that Mr. Burke has as
little refpect for truth, as he has for humanity in affliction. But the object of this note has no relation with
the fad deftiny, guilt, or innocence of M. de la Fayette :
its purport is to reprobate and expofe the fcandalous
expedient of a man (poffeffed of a certain degree of po-
pularity and a fhew of talents) playing with the paffions
and prejudices of the multitude, and practifing on the
eafy credulity of the people, every defpicable artifice that
can bewilder their judgment, or degrade their capacities.
It is not private hiftory that I mean to inveftigate ; but
the impudent profligacy and arrogance of a man in public
life, who has the effrontery to hold himfelf out as a model
of loyalty. Faulty, reprehenfible, and marked by an infi-
nity of low cunning, as his private life may be, it is be-
neath my cenfure or regard. I will not conjure from the
filent manfions of the dead the ghofts of departed friends!
Peace to the venerable and lamented manes of Saunders,
Rockingham, and Reynolds !—Peace to the haplefs injured fhades of Verney and of Hargrave, let them fleep
in

dities and impudence, gave a colourable
pretext to an herd of fcribblers to arraign

the

in quiet; they can neither be cozened nor IMPEACH-
ED! I will not rake among *their* afhes, left I fhould be
compelled to call for *civet to fweeten my imagination.* But
when a man comes forward in a public chara&ter, in-
vefted with a public truft, he challenges our notice, and
muft abide the fcrutiny. Mr. Burke has ill deferved the
reputation he has acquired, and his pretenfions to confequence are lefs founded than his claims to merit. The
world appears to have been fteady in its judgment, and to
have formed a juft eftimate of the value of this bufy and
officious meddler, until the epoch of the French revolution, when, frightened on the firft alarm, it trembled for
the event, and without being in danger of drowning,
caught at each ftraw that paffed. It is fometimes profitable to fpeculate ; and where the reward is confiderable,
and the rifque trifling, the prudence of the adventurer
will feldom be impeached. Mr. Burke has not paffed
through life an entire ftranger to fpeculations of this defcription ; and if Beaconsfield could boaft its archives,
we fhould find records, perhaps, that fome of his enter-
prifes have been more fortunate than *judicious.* The period, however, which has been the moft fingularly
marked by favour, and in which with the *leaft defert* he

has

the purity of thofe political tenets which,
decorating with all the fanctity of religion,

has gained the *moft renown*, is that of the period to
which I have already alluded. The houfe of Cavendifh,
compelled from neceffity to adopt a fyftem of œconomy,
in the arrangements of which the maintenance of men-
dicant legiflators could have no fhare, did not hold out
any pleafing affurances, that the evening of his life would
be as comfortable as its meridian had been brilliant.
The Duke of Portland, without totally abandoning the
hope that his fpeculations would yield moft profitable
returns, became lefs zealous for what he had little chance
of obtaining; and under thefe diftreffing circumftances
it is poffible that Mr. Burke firft conceived the idea of renouncing his old friends and connections, and to expect,
by veering completely round to the oppofite point of the
compafs, to come in for a fhare of the good things in
this world, which he faw very little profpect of acquiring on the credit of his own name and pretenfions.
While he had an hope that thofe with whom he acted
would again come into power he continued with them;
but the inftant he difcerned the little chance of Eden being once more opened to their view, he realized the fable
of the rats and the finking fhip, and left them to fhift for
themfelves. No man, I believe, better underftands a bar-
gain,

gion, he would have impofed upon us as
an orthodox creed, from which it would be

the

gain, either in grofs or detail, than this gentleman; while,
verfed in the hiftory of the paffions, he is perfect mafter
of the ebbs and flows of our affections, and well knows
how to traffic in thofe of others, without rifque or injury to his own. Mr. Burke has with equal juftice and
feverity cenfured J. J. Roufleau for the unnatural defertion of his helplefs and illegitimate offspring : but
what fhall we fay to this folemn and inflexible judge of
mankind, when we behold him throwing off without
provocation, compunction, forrow, or regret, ancient
and long eftablifhed intimacies—fpurning with difdain,
and renouncing all former ties, and all thofe friend-
fhips which we imagined were confirmed and confo-
lidated by the ftrongeft of all moral cements, intereft,
gratitude, and misfortune?—How comes it that all thefe
fentiments and relations, tender, impreffive, and endearing as they have ever been with other men, have
had fuch little hold on the mind of this man that they
in one fhort moment were violently broken down, torn,
burft afunder, trampled on, and diffolved, leaving neither
trace nor veftige, even in his remembrance to mark
their former exiftence?

What

the height of impiety if not blafphemy to depart.

This

What a leffon for men acting together in great public concerns! What a leffon to men engaged or defirous to engage in parties! while mankind in general may pro-fit by the admonition it offers, and the proof it affords of the very little fhare which the heart has in the friend-fhips of this world! Why did Mr. Burke defert men with whom he had fo long acted in common concert, for whom he had uniformly profeffed the warmeft at-tachment, whofe meafures he fupported and applauded, till even flattery fickened at the fulfome panegyric?— What fair and juft motives could he have urged in 1793 for fuch defertion, that would not have applied and have been equally valid in 1783? At this latter period' he was difpofed to go all lengths with thofe whofe con-duct was certainly not lefs reprehenfible than it is at prefent: and he continued to act with them on occa-fions where a good man with moderate parts would have paufed; where a virtuous and ftrong mind would have refufed; and in which a corrupt one only would have joined. If this converfion or apoftacy—for I will not, in mercy to the gentleman's faith and religion, call it *recantation*—is the natural and unconftrained movements of his confcience, how comes it that this

ufeful

· This Gentleman, by his overstrained devotion, brought the whole fabric of our political

useful but neglected monitor, now so easily alarmed, allowed him to join in the conspiracy that would have stolen the diadem from the head of Majesty, to have placed it in appearance on that of his misguided son, while those about him defaced or pilfered its richest ornaments and jewels? Is it to make his peace with the sovereign whom he insulted, that he chants hymns of loyalty and psalms of gladness, morning, noon, and night? It is unnecessary; for resentment cannot exist where the virtues reside. Is it to improve a fortune, fabricated God knows how, that he pays court to authority, and, spaniel-like, licks the hand that cuffed him? I have no objection. It is perfectly indifferent to me whether he speculates in the funds or in places. Let him obtain lucrative employments for another, and reserve the emoluments for himself; the profits will enable him to improve his plantations at Beaconsfield, and to crimson still deeper with an additional glass of good Port the rosy cheeks of his venerable confessor: but do not let him in the abundance of his zeal injure those for whom he has expressed an attachment as novel as it is extraordinary; do not let him provoke a legion

N   of

political religion (if I may fo exprefs myfelf) into hazard—hence the virulence
with

of unprincipled fcribblers to debauch, corrupt, and poi-
fon the public mind, with doctrines and maxims fub-
verfive of all order. Let him, for Heaven's fake, be
difcouraged from furnifhing weapons (by overftrained
arguments and grofs mifreprefentations) to Treafon and
Sedition to affail our wife and happy eftablifhments in
Church and State.

I aver it to be a fact, felt and acknowledged by every
gentleman, without exception, with whom I have con-
verfed on the fubject, men of whofe loyalty and attachment no doubt can be entertained, that it was the Reflections of Mr. Burke on the French Revolution that
gave birth to the Rights of Man, Pig's Meat, and other
atrocious, abominable publications, which have had a
moft rapid and extenfive fale among that clafs of people the moft eafily inflamed, and who have ultimately
the moft mifchief to apprehend from civil tumult and
diforder.

I am firmly convinced that if Mr. Burke had not produced his book of various hues, for it is even tinged
with that Jacobinifm which it pretends to decry, that
the pamphlets and libels with which the laws of this
country

with which it was affailed by a man more
diftinguifhed by his misfortunes than his
talents,

country have been braved and infringed, would never
have appeared: and for Mr. Burke to come forward with
the entire hiftory of his political life frefh in our remembrance, was an infult to our underftanding, and as
indifferent a proof of his modefty as it is of his fincerity. This want of confiftency argues want of principle, and is much nearer allied to fraud and profligacy than to weaknefs or error. We trace the cloven
foot and leprous mind of the author in almoft
every line of his book; the features of its parent are
eafily difcovered; and we behold the legitimate offspring
of truant Vice, returned penitent and afhamed of having
been feduced into the paths of Virtue and of Honour.
That the public, however, may the better eftimate the
conduct and principles of this gentleman, I have annexed
complete fentences from different fpeeches in Parliament, which prove that he was very folicitous at fome
periods of his life, and when it fuited his purpofe, to
bring the people forward from that back ground, into
which he would now drive and pound them, like ftrayed
fheep. Thofe whom he would now confider as form-
ing no part, and having neither rights nor influence,

N 2   were

talents, and who feems to have braved
the public opinion with an effrontery
bordering

were formerly of fome account; and, in his opinion,
" *their fenfe was to govern the legiflature of this country.*"
That I may not be accufed of giving partial mutilated
extracts, for the unfair purpofe of holding him out to
that public for fentence or acquittal to which he has
fo often appealed for judgment againft others, I have
given the dates to each quotation; for it is not by ill-
founded affertions and declamations, but by facts, that
I mean to prove the little claim which he has to confidence or fupport; nor fhall any confideration on earth
force or feduce me to relinquifh the vantage ground I
have obtained, until I have curbed his infolence or corrected his propenfities.

" The *rights of men*, that is to fay, the natural rights
of mankind, are indeed facred things; and if any public
meafure is proved mifchievoufly to affect them, the objection ought to be fatal to that meafure, even if no
charter at all could be fet up againft it.

" If thefe natural rights are further affirmed and declared by exprefs covenants, if they are clearly defined
and fecured againft chicane, againft power, and authority, by written inftruments and pofitive engagements,
they are in a ftill better condition; they partake not
only

bordering upon infanity. If Mr. Burke,
by his late wilful mifreprefentation of the
principles

only of the fanctity of the object fo fecured, but of
that folemn public faith itfelf, which fecures an object
of fuch importance. Indeed this formal recognition,
by the fovereign power, of an original right in the fubject,
can never be fubverted, but *by rooting up the holding ra-
dical principles of government, and even of fociety itfelf."*—
Speech on Mr. Fox's Eaft India Bill, Dec. 1, 1783,
quarto edition, page 331.

" It muft be granted to me that all political power
which is fet over men, and that all privilege claimed or
exercifed in exclufion of them, being wholly *artificial,*
and for fo much a derogation from the natural *equality*
of mankind at large, ought to be fome way or other
exercifed ultimately for their benefit.—If this is true
with regard to every fpecies of political dominion, and
every defcription of commercial privilege, none of
which can be *original felf-derived rights, or grants for the
mere private benefit of the holders**, then fuch rights or
privileges,

* Let this paffage be contrafted with the following extract, which Mr. Burke has cited in his Appeal from the
New to the Old Whigs, for the purpofe of combating and
refuting it, without doing either ; and it will appear that
the

principles on which the Englifh Revolution was happily accomplifhed in the
laft

privileges, or whatever elfe you choofe to call them, are
all in the ftrictefl fenfe a TRUST ; and it is in the very
effence of every truft to be rendered ACCOUNTABLE,
and even totally to *ceafe*, when it fubftantially varies
from the purpofes for which alone it could have a
lawful exiftence.

" This I conceive, fir, to be true of trufts of power
vefled in the higheft hands, and of fuch as feem to hold
of no human creature."—Speech on Mr. Fox's Eaft
India Bill, Dec. 1, 1783, quarto edition, page 333.

" I ground myfelf therefore on this principle—*that
if the abufe is proved, the contract is broken; and we re-
enter into all our rights;* that is, into the exercife of all
our duties.—Our own authority indeed is as much a

the fentiment correfponds precifely with what that gentleman
advanced in the Houfe of Commons at a period many years
antecedent to the publication he cenfures; and which might
have been called at that time, " The Rights of Man, by
Edmund Burke."—" *What is government more than the management of the affairs of a nation ? It is not, and from its nature
cannot be the property of any particular man or family, but of the
whole community, at whofe expence it is fupported.*"—Extract
from Paine's Rights of Man, in the Appeal from the New to
the Old Whigs, quarto edition, page 463.

truft

laft century, did not juftify the licentioufnefs of Mr. Paine, he certainly provoked
the

truft originally, as the Company's authority is a truft
derivatively ; and it is the ufe we make of the refumed
power that muft juftify or condemn us in the refumption
of it."—Speech on Mr. Fox's Eaft India Bill, Dec. 1,
1783, quarto edition, page 334.

" Much had been faid of the fenfe of the people, as
the grounds on which minifters might reft their defence
of the late diffolution; and on this head I am ready to
confefs, that *the fenfe of the people, however erroneous at
times, muft always govern the legiflature of this country."*
—Parliamentary Debates, June 14, 1784.

" Allufions have upon this occafion been made
to the Revolution and the Reftoration ; but they
were acts of neceffity, having attendant upon them,
their peculiar ways ; but what was the nature of
the Revolution, and what was the nature of the reftraints upon the executive power, agreed upon and
confented to, at that memorable period? They were
thefe :—*If a king fhall abolifh or alter courts of law, trial
by jury, or religion, or erect a ftanding army ; then the compact is* DISSOLVED, *and all right and power reverts
to the people*—and the people by PLOTS, CONSPI-
RACIES,

the ftrictures and animadverfions of that
wretched incendiary, and let loofe a legion
of

RACIES, or any other SECRET or VIOLENT *means*
may HURL fuch a king from the throne.—The Revolution was in fact a precedent of a DELINQUENT
monarch, a precedent to teach this leffon to kings :

"Difcite Juftitiam moniti, et non temnere Leges."

Debates on the Regency, Monday, Dec. 22, 1788.

It may perhaps be thought that I have treated Mr.
Burke with uncommon afperity ; but I have only dealt
the fame meafure to him that he has dealt to others ;
and while retaliation partakes of the nature of equity,
my ftrictures cannot be condemned, nor can he in decency complain of feeling in his turn a portion of that
feverity which he has exercifed at various times with
fuch extreme rancour againft feveral of the ableft and
moft virtuous characters in the kingdom. I will not
appeal to the fufpicious and equivocal teftimony of thofe
with whom he has acted, nor of thofe whom he has
oppofed, but to the incontrovertible evidence of expe
rience. It is to the unerring judgment of mankind that
I appeal, whether the whole of his public conduct has
not been contradictory and inconfiftent, wafpifh, impe-

ı   rious

of firebrands in the country, who de-
grading our moral worth as well as our
mental

rious and vindictive ? whether he is not to be traced
through all the serpentine windings of his political ex-
istence, by the poison he has trailed and the mischiefs
he has occasioned ? And is it for this man, hated, de-
spised, and deserted as he is by all parties, to elevate his
voice, at once the Stentor and the Mentor of the age ?
Is it this man, this *Pope* in politics, who is at variance
with himself and with all the world, that pretends to in-
fallibility ? who, fixing bells to his own neck, flies off
in a direct tangent, expecting us to follow him over
hedges and ditches, the bell-wether of the flock; leap-
ing without why or wherefore the fences of wisdom,
prudence, right, justice, and humanity ? For Heaven's
sake, what are the pretensions of this extraordinary per-
sonage, that he should arrogate so much to himself and
allow so little to others ? What is there in his conduct
to admire or to imitate ? and with what credit to morals,
or with what safety to the public interest, can his elo-
quence, however splendid, vehement and forcible, be
urged in extenuation of what even Mildness in her best
humour would refuse to class under the head either of
absurdity or inconsistency ? Is an imagination, inflamed

O   to

mental faculties, would have iſſued from
their High Court of Chancery ſtatutes
of

to madneſs by flattery, and in which metaphors are
crowded with as gaudy a profuſion as we ſee mirrors
diſplayed in the ſhop of a carver and gilder, to dazzle,
corrupt and blind our better underſtanding?—No man
is more diſpoſed than myſelf to pay the juſt tribute of
applauſe to diſtinguiſhed talents and virtues; but I cannot contemplate the abilities of Mr. Burke, without
drawing a compariſon very much to his diſadvantage,
between their *excellence* and their *application*. Such
has been the reſult of my obſervations on a man whoſe
conduct in public life I have followed very cloſely; and
as one of the jury impanelled to decide on the public
proceedings of men in public ſituations, I am under no
apprehenſion that my veracity or judgment will be impeached by the verdict I have given.

I owe this explanation not to the ſorry object in
queſtion, but to the Miniſter, who may perhaps think it
extraordinary that I ſhould grapple a man with ſuch
fierceneſs, who has of late ſupported the meaſures of
the Crown with an ardour and enthuſiaſm equal to my
own. No man can poſſibly have a more exalted opinion of the talents and rectitude of Mr. Pitt, than I have.

What

of lunacy and bankruptcy againſt every
deſcription of ſocieties and government,
but thoſe of their own conſtruction.

In

What his father ſaid of the late Lord Clive as a General, may with ſtill greater juſtice be applied to the firſt
of theſe as a Miniſter; but my veneration cannot exempt
me from other duties which I feel myſelf bound to ful-
fil, nor need he be aſhamed of the panegyric of a man
who is ſuperior to the infamy of writing for hire, and
who diſdains to flatter or deceive. My object in enabling
the world to form a juſt eſtimate of Mr. Burke's character, is to diſqualify him for future hoſtility. My
intention is to furniſh an antidote to the venom he
diſtils with a profuſion ſufficient to infect the general
maſs of humanity, and to render this Miſchief to the
country as harmleſs to the Government which he injures
and inſults by his ſupport, as he is contemptible. Nor
can I fail. I muſt eventually triumph, for the pro-
greſs of truth, though ſlow, is certain; its influence,
however counteracted by art or oppoſed by violence, is
irreſiſtible and permanent, while that of deluſion is, as
it ought to be, ſhort, precarious, and tranſitory. Hence
the hope and conſolation, which afflicted perſecuted
excellence derives under the preſſure of unmerited and

aggra-

In allowing us fo fmall a portion of intellect, and a ftill lefs portion of knowledge, Mr. Paine would reduce us to a ftate of childhood, imbecillity, and infolvency; he feems to have confidered all mankind as in their infancy, and fuppofing himfelf alone arrived at maturity, would have claimed and exercifed as a right, the guardianfhip of the whole human race. How far he may be qualified for fo important a tafk, may be collected from the hiftory of his life; and though we may fmile at the folly of prefcribing to the world the conduct it fhould obferve, we cannot but reprobate the infolence that would ufurp a dominion over

aggravated oppreffion. Hence the great fecurity which mankind enjoy and poffefs againft every defcription of fraud, as well as againft the craft and ambition of grave and folemn impoftors, however dignified, rewarded, or protected they may be by the miftaken policy of the Court.

our

[125]

our minds, and reduce us to a state of mental servitude, more deplorable in prospect, and more humiliating and horrible in its effects, than the despotism he declaimed against.

There is always an obligation due to bad men, whenever they reveal their intentions. Presuming upon the lenity of our laws, more than upon the equity of his designs, Mr. Paine came forward with a boldness that eclipses even the licence of modern times, and proposed to an entire nation enjoying perfect tranquillity from without, and perfect security within—to a nation in a state of prosperity unexampled in the history of mankind, and happy in its Government, a total subversion of its Laws and Constitution!

Such a proposition at any other season would be treated with ridicule, and the man who made it supposed to have escaped

3

caped from Bedlam; but at this moment, and in the ferment that agitates men's minds on the Continent, it is turpitude, not infanity, inafmuch as it aims to accomplifh the mifchiefs it recommends, and would involve an entire country and people in ruin. His efforts were not directed againft any particular Government, but againft all Governments; they were not new regulations that he would eftablifh, but old ones that he would abolifh. Order was to have been fubverted, not preferved, and war declared, not againft Priefts or Sovereigns, not againft Superftition or Defpotifm, not againft Monarchy, Ariftocracy, or Republicanifm, but againft Civil Society in general, and under whatever form it may exift.

The whole human race was included in this terrible profcription; and from this wild and ruthlefs chaos of accumulated

lated crimes and follies, you pretend, my Lord, that Wifdom and Juftice would arife, and baftardize their parents!

It is vexatious in the extreme to fee talents that might prove ufeful to mankind fo fhamefully perverted. The ftrong and comprehenfive powers you poffefs entitle your Lordfhip to a diftinguifhed rank in fociety : but while we reverence your abilities, we lament, as a misfortune to yourfelf and others, that your difcretion and rectitude (we mean rectitude in argument, for it does not become us to notice any other) fhould bear no proportion to the genius and activity of your mind. The publications to which I allude, as far as they relate to the Laws and Government of this country, are not only a direct attack upon the Conftitution, but upon the conduct and principles of the Nation at large ! They are as much a libel on the good fenfe and integrity of the

People,

People, as on the King, Lords, and Commons.

They not only affert that the Reprefentation is defective, the Peerage ufelefs, and the Monarchy burthenfome and difgraceful, but that we are accomplices in the guilt that plunders and infults us. It is not ufual, my Lord, to traduce thofe whom we would perfuade or win to our purpofe; nor is it the fureft method to make men think highly of the force and extent of their faculties, by depreciating their underftanding.

To convert us by abufing us, is, as far as my reading and experience enable me to judge, unprecedented in controverfy, and more likely to confirm than to remove error; but whatever may be the motive, the manner is offenfive, and the attempt dangerous.

The peace and profperity, my Lord, of ten millions of your fellow creatures (I had almoft

almoft called them by the more endearing
name of countrymen) are not even regarded
as fecondary confiderations by Mr. Paine *

and

* There is not a more pleafing fubject for contem-
plation to virtuous and benevolent minds than the
progrefs of reafon from infancy to maturity. It is the
genuine and animating route of knowledge, which it is
impoffible to behold or follow at any period of our
lives without advantage to ourfelves and others. It is
the converfion of ignorance, by gradual and effectual
means, to wifdom, and it is probable that a very trifling
attention to the procefs might have improved the morals and corrected the underftanding of Mr. Paine. But the
mild and ufeful arts of peace appear to have no hold on
his affections ; they have nothing in them correfpon-
dent with the ftrange and difcordant nature of his ambition ; and no fooner was tranquillity eftablifhed in
the weftern hemifphere, than he flew to Europe with
the rapidity of thought in purfuit of frefh adventures.
He difcarded his adopted child America, with as little
regret as he abandoned England, his venerable parent
country, and renouncing with an unnatural apathy
every obligation of filial duty—every fenfe of paternal
goodnefs—renouncing even all focial intercourfe with

P

the

and his affociates; they were not taken into the fcheme of his benevolence, not even

the world, and every tie that links man to man in the great confederacy of Nations, we find him by choice, not neceffity, a peor and forry outcaft—a vagrant on the furface of the globe, without a country or an home to fly to, immured within the gloomy walls of a prifon, and menaced with a death as ignominious as his life, by the very wretches, whofe patronage he courted, and whofe crimes he idolized.   To an active and well dif-pofed mind, America prefented a wide and delightful field for fpeculation and honeft induftry. His genius, however extenfive it may be, would have found ample occupation on that vaft continent, and pofterity might have been indebted to his zeal and his talents for com-forts and improvements unknown to the prefent time. If the real interefts of mankind had been the purfuit of this miferable, degraded and worthlefs object; if it had ferioufly been his wifh to diffufe the light of reafon over every part of the earth; how comes it that the unenlightened and uncivilized tribes in the internal parts of America were not comprehended in that fcheme of univerfal fraternity and felicity which he profeffes fo vehemently in converfation and in print, but violates in practice ?

even as a contingency. On the contrary,
we were required to engage in riot and
revolt,

practice ? How comes it that thofe equal rights which
he took fo much pains to communicate to the intelli-
gent and cultivated European, were not revealed to the
untutored Indian, and a benevolent effort made on his
part to reclaim whole nations from the ignorance and
ferocious barbarifm in which they have been enveloped
from the birth of time ? If it is his ambition to collect
and harmonize the difperfed and vagrant inhabitants of
the earth into focial intercourfe with each other, the
back fettlements of that vaft country, which his vanity
pretends to have liberated and illumined, would have
afforded abundant employment for his zeal, as well as
ample exercife for his genius and induftry. The im-
menfe and almoft impenetrable forefts in the weftern
world might, by his exertions, have given place in a few
years to populous towns and cities ;—the pathlefs wild
through which the wretched Indian explores his folitary way might have been converted into fruitful and
well-cultivated plains, and the rude and haplefs natives
changed from favages into citizens and men !—A well-
ordered Government might have arifen in the defert ;
and ruthlefs, predatory war have given way to peace,

fecurity,

revolt, not for our own particular advantage, but for that of others—for that of
our

fecurity, and comfort. But the wretched ftate of conftant and ferocious hoftility approaches nearer to his
ideas of natural right, and better fuits the coarfe and
barbarous texture of his mind. The fcalping-knife levelled at a chief gives him the idea of an axe raifed
againft his Sovereign. It falls in unifon with his principles and his feelings, and leaves him nothing to covet
or enjoy. Difdaining all decency and referve, he avows
in the face of the world, that it is the fubverfion, not
the formation of States at which he aims. The din of
civil difcord alone vibrates fweet mufic to his ear, and
domeftic, not foreign war is his object. The conflict
of contending Nations has nothing in it sufficiently mifchievous or fanguinary to engage his notice. The repelling of unprovoked hoftility or of wanton invafion can
neither awaken his attention nor deferve his applaufe;
but when Rebellion rears its terrific head above the level
and controul of law; when the bloody arm of the
fubject is raifed againft his legitimate Prince, and that
of the child againft the author of his exiftence, Mr.
Paine feels interefted in the event; and, anticipating the
fall of Kings, Magiftrates, and Laws! the extinction of
virtue,

our inveterate enemies, my Lord ; and if
any good, contrary to all probability, had
refulted

virtue, juſtice, and humanity, he riots in the ruin he
beholds, and declares the millennium at hand.   It
is not the patriotic reſiſtance of independent States to
foreign oppreſſion that charms and fooths his foul, but
private feuds grown into inſurrection and anarchy.
Where decrepid age, fcarce able to fuftain its tottering
weight under the combined preſſure of age and infirmities, receives from fome obfcure aſſaſſin its final difmif-
fion from the world!   where the citizen is armed
againſt citizen—brother againſt brother—and the fon
againſt his venerable and affrighted parent! where all
right is confounded, and all ages, fexes, and conditions,
involved in one general and comprehenfive ruin ! Such
are the fcenes that rouze him into action ! fuch the
purfuits that afford guilty occupation and amufement
to his reſtleſs mind.

Happily his career of infamy has been interrupted
by his accomplices in crime.   Defpifed, fufpected and .
imprifoned by his fanguinary aſſociates, he has no longer the power of doing mifchief; and glad to compound
on any terms for a life fcarce worth preferving, he is
likely to terminate his wretched exiſtence in a jail ! Let
thofe

refulted from our guilt and folly, we were
not certain of being permitted to enjoy
it; for the object of the anarchy and
confufion into which we were to be pre-
cipitated was to give peace and fecurity to
France, not happinefs and profperity to
England. No benefit was promifed as a
boon beforehand, or as a recompenfe afterwards. No flattering hope was held out
to us even in perfpective, or any equiva-
lent offered for relinquifhing prefent eafe
and comfort, and facrificing at a venture,
and for no one poffible good to ourfelves, all
that renders life defirable or fupportable.
Surely, my Lord, you muft have departed
from your accuftomed prudence, as well
as from every idea of duty and refpect to

thofe who approving of his conduct would adopt his principles be admonifhed by his fate. Let his hiftory and
cataftrophe be impreffed on their minds, and engraven
on their hearts; for there is wifdom in the leffon, which
it may be imprudent if not hazardous to fpurn.

5

mankind,

mankind, when you urged us to gua-
rantee rapine, profcription, and maffacre
in France.

After having felled to the ground with
more than Gothic barbarity all that was
good or dignified; after having mowed
down with remorfelefs rage all that was
venerable and exalted in their wretched
and diftracted country; after having rioted
in flaughter, till even carnage, gorged
without being fatiated, fickens at the hor-
rid banquet, the favage villains, ftill co-
vetous of blood, are hewing each other
down with as much fury and expedition
as they butchered their fuperiors. And
yet, my Lord, terrible as this wild and ferocious conflict is even to the imagination;
fanguinary and unexampled as it is in
the annals of our nature, and in which
nothing appears but a diabolical emulation
for a pre-eminence in guilt; your Lordship

ſhip avowedly ſtands forth an admirer of crimes which deſolate the earth and diſhonour humanity! Are we, then, to become a rampart to iniquity; the bondſmen of aſſaſſins and of public robbers? of men immerſed in every ſpecies of guilt that degrades manhood, and renders this world a wildernefs of crimes?

Muſt we, in conjunction with other nations, my Lord, form a ring-fence as it were round France, while, loſt to all ſenſe of honour and of virtue, ſhe revels in every ſpecies of enormity with impunity, and ſets religion and morals at defiance? It is ſcarce within the ſcope and reach of thought that ſuch an expectation could exiſt in any well-organized brain, much leſs that it ſhould be expreſſed and publicly avowed. Yet ſuch is the expectation that your Lordſhip has ventured to form; it ſtands recorded in your parliamentary harangues,

rangues, unencumbered by conditions and unaccompanied by any affurance of national benefit to us in return.

As far as fuch an avowal puts us on our guard, and enables us to counteract intended mifchief, we are obliged to your Lordfhip; but are you aware, my Lord, that you are giving us in your legiflative capacity a comment on Mr. Paine, in whofe text an antipathy to Kings and Peers is not only expreffed, but a pofitive declaration avowed, in direct terms, that " *France muſt be furrounded with revolutions* " *before ſhe will be in peace and fafety?*"

And is it for this folitary purpofe that we are called upon with an effrontery unexampled in the hiftory of libellous and feditious publications, to renounce not only the Conftitution and Government under which we happily live, but to relinquifh our prejudices, our attachments, and affections, to throw them from us as

Q   aliens,

aliens, and as enemies unworthy of notice
or regard; to renounce all that education,
duty, and habit have imprinted on our
hearts and minds; and to give up without
a pang or a figh all thofe tender and endearing ties that bind us to each other,
and conftitute the very charm of exiftence? Even the obligations of religion,
facred and immutable as they are, are expected to fall in this intended general
wreck, and what connects us as it were
with heaven and eternity, relinquifhed
and denied! Are you aware, my Lord,
that at this moment a " *peace of France*"
(for which you feem fo indecently anxious) can be obtained on no other terms
than by a war with reafon and humanity?
And muft her felicity be purchafed by
fo much forrow and aggravated calamity?
Muft the extinction of the various nations
in Europe be the price of her exiftence
and fecurity? And can her repofe be
found

found only in the defpondency and ruin of the human race? Fie upon it, my Lord!

The imagination ftartles at the idea; and it may well be afked in what infernal feminary of foul and prepofterous guilt you have been fchooled into fuch maxims of right and humanity? Let us fuppofe, my Lord, that the Government you have declaimed againft, not that which you admire, was fubverted. Imagine to yourfelf the wreck and diffolution of the various parts which confolidate its power, while they fupport and dignify each other. Imagine to yourfelf (for the picture is not overcharged) a fanguinary rabble let loofe from all reftraint; our wealthy and numerous manufacturers difperfed; their looms, forges, and mills deftroyed; their habitations pillaged and their perfons profcribed! Behold their haplefs wives and unoffending offspring forlorn and pennylefs, turned out on the wild

Q 2

and

and ruthlefs common, menaced with fa-
mine, and compelled to folicit death as an
act of mercy from the hands of affaffins
ftained with the blood of their hufbands
and their fathers! Imagine the accom-
plifhment of all thefe aggravated horrors,
my Lord, and you will have a faint idea
of what would refult from the adoption
of your councils, and the introduction of
thofe maxims and principles which you
admire in a nation that has every claim
to your refentment, for having poifoned
your mind with fentiments which I truft
are as foreign to your nature as they are
unworthy of your rank and education.
Amidft fuch complicated horrors, amidft
fuch fcenes of rueful wafte and defolation,
without power, without fortune, credit,
or influence, expofed to infult, and a men-
dicant for your life as well as for your
fubfiftence to the very men who are
become mafters of both—what would
be

be your reflections? what would be your
fituation? to whom would you fly for
protection? where would you feek refuge, not from the ruin that ftares you
in the face, and cannot be avoided, but
from the bitter and agonifing reproaches
of your own confcience? Under fuch
diftreffing circumftances, you might perhaps for a fhort time evade the fatal
ftroke that would terminate at once your
fufferings and exiftence; but though you
could fly from the poignard, though a
refinement in cruelty might afford you a
refpite for a few days or weeks, I will
defy you to fly from *yourfelf*. Your reflections, fharpened by remorfe as well as
by a fenfe of your own lamentable and
deplorable condition, would harafs and
purfue you; and, anticipating the juft
vengeance of Heaven, give your Lordfhip a tolerable idea of that hell which
religion has affigned to the guilty.

My

My Lord, I would entreat you to excufe the freedom with which I have ad-
dreffed you, but the importance of my
fubject is an apology for my warmth: and
I am unwilling to believe that you can be
offended with a man, whofe motives, however ungracious his manner may be, are
laudable, and who certainly has no other
object in view, than to deftroy, if poffible,
the delufion under which you have acted,
and to revive in your breaft that ardent zeal
for the intereft of your country, which
marked the infancy of your parliamentary
career. I know that you have been deceived—I know that you entertained an
opinion that Mr. Maret was authorifed to
treat with Mr. Pitt in November 1792 ; and
that the War might have been avoided if
the Minifter had entered into a negociation
with that gentleman. This opinion became
general, and hence the torrent of abufe which
flowed in every direction againft Government,

ment, and bore down for a time the good fenfe and juſtice of the country. It is to the influence of this impreſſion that I attribute the part which your Lordſhip has taken of late in public affairs, and the acrimony with which you accuſe Adminiſtration with being the authors of a war, which Mr. Maret, the night I had the honour to fee your Lordſhip at his apartments in Portman Square, might have aſſured you it was not in their power to have avoided. But that gentieman was lefs explicit with your Lord-ſhip than he was with me; nor did the Executive Council at Paris repoſe much more confidence in their Agent, than he appears to have done in your Lordſhip. At the period above mentioned he had no authority to folicit an interview with Mr. Pitt, or to treat on the affairs of the two nations. His miſſion to England was of a private nature, and entirely confined to fome domeſtic arrangements in the family of the late

8   Duke

Duke of Orleans. That he fhould, thus circumftanced, have had a conference with Mr. Pitt, may well appear extraordinary to your Lordfhip; and having obtained an interview with the Minifter, it was fair to conclude that he had come over exprefsly for the purpofe. I will explain the enigma by informing your Lordfhip, that this conference was the refult of that fpirit of intrigue which reigns with more or lefs vehemence in all his countrymen. London at that time was crowded with a number of political adventurers, who were at once friends, enemies, fpies, rivals, and informers againft each other: all of them pretended to be Agents from the Executive Council; and one of thefe embryo Ambaffadors, afpiring to the honour of fuperfeding Mr. Chauvelin, announced himfelf as the perfon authorifed to treat privately with the Britifh Minifter. He repeatedly declared that he had fomething of confequence to communicate from

Mr.

Mr. Le Brun; and preffing with unremitting zeal and affiduity for an interview, a confidential friend of Mr. Pitt was deputed to receive the propofitions of this pretended agent: but when the parties met, it was not *this* man but *another* that was deputed to treat. That other, my Lord, was Mr. Maret; and when he was produced from behind the curtain, it appeared that he had as little to fay as his friend, and that neither was inftructed to open any negociation, or to offer any propofitions whatever to Government. Your Lordfhip will eafily believe that an interview obtained by trick, and that could lead to nothing, was not very long; neither could the converfation that paffed be very interefting. Mr. Maret having nothing to fay, contented himfelf with expreffing the happinefs he fhould feel in being inftrumental in preferving a good underftanding between the two nations, and after a few general expreffions of a fimilar nature

R   he

he retired. This was his frank acknowledgment to me at the time, and he has even declared it to me in his correspondence, in consequence of some letters that passed between us in the interval, on the subject of the deceit that had been practised by his precursor, and on the impudence of Le Brun, who, on receiving information of this interview, went down to the National Convention and assured them that "*the English Minister had* PROVOKED *a conference with one of their secret agents, but that he had been peremptorily forbidden to open himself any farther to Mr. Pitt, or to have any further intercourse whatever with him, either directly or indirectly, on public affairs.*" I read the dispatch with equal indignation and surprise, for it contained expressions as indecent as they were unjust and arrogant: and on my pointing out to Mr. Maret the inferences that might be drawn from the falsehood of afferting that the conference to which he had

been

been admitted, was at the *inſtance* of Mr. Pitt; he obſerved they were mere words of courſe, the ill interpretation of which it ſhould be his care to correct on his return to France. It is of little conſequence to enquire whether this aſſertion, ſo void of truth, originated with him, or with Le Brun; all I mean to infer from ſtating the fact, is, that little dependance can be placed on the evidence of men capable of ſuch miſrepreſentation. It is now incumbent on me to convince your Lordſhip that the former perſon had no public miſſion to this country at the time that he obtained an interview with Mr. Pitt; and as a proof that I do not advance what I cannot eſtabliſh, I refer your Lordſhip to an extract from a letter which I received from Mr. Maret, dated Paris, January 11, 1793, and which I am at liberty to publiſh, *without being guilty of a breach of confidence.* It was in conſequence of my expreſſing myſelf with ſome acrimony, at

the

the conduct of Le Brun, and the fraudulent
artifice by which the interview with Mr. Pitt
was obtained.—It is as follows:

" Dites moi donc nettement, mon cher
" Miles, quels font vos fujets de plaintes?
" S'agirait-il de quelques inexactitudes qui fe
" font gliffés dans le rapport que Le Brun a
" fait avant que je fuffe de retour à Paris?
" Je conviens avec vous que fon énonciation
" fur les conférences de nos agens fecrets
" n'eft pas exacte—Je n'étais point AGENT
" SECRET——je n'avais ni AUTORI-
" SATION—NI MISSION, & j'ai dit la
" vérité en le declarant à vous, et à Mr. Pitt
" ——Le Miniftre s'eft trompé, & je n'ai
" trompé ni vous ni Mr. Pitt——Dieu vous
" garde de la foupçonner, fi mon amitié vous
" eft chere! car je fens qu'elle ne furvivrait pas
" à un foupçon injurieux dont ma délicateffe
" et ma bonnefoi feraient frappés———Au
" refte, mon cher Miles, ne nous occupons

4   " pas

" pas de ces triftes idées, et ne fongeons qu'à

" l'intérêt que nous mettons réciproquement

" à être toujours amis.—

(Signé) "HUGUES BERNARD MARET."*

* " PARIS, 11th January, 1793.

" Tell me then freely, my dear Miles, what are the
" grounds of your complaint againft me? Is it on ac-
" count of the inaccuracies which appeared in the report
" that Le Brun made before my return?—I agree with
" you that his ftatement of the conferences with our
" fecret agents is not exact.—I was not a fecret agent
" —I had no authority to treat, nor had I any miffion;
" and in declaring this to Mr. Pitt and to yourfelf, I ac-
" knowledged nothing but the truth.—

" The Minifter (Le Brun) deceived himfelf, but I
" neither deceived you nor Mr. Pitt. If my friendfhip
" is dear to you, God preferve you from harbouring
" fuch an opinion! for I feel very fenfibly, that it will
" not furvive a fufpicion fo injurious, which would
" equally wound my delicacy and my fincerity—Banifh
" then, my dear Miles, thofe painful ideas, and think
" only of that zeal, and that intereft which we mutually
" feel to continue in friendfhip with each other.

(Signed)   "HUGUES BERNARD MARET."

Your

Your Lordſhip will perceive from the above extract that Mr. Maret had no public miſſion to this country in 1792; and you might have learnt from himſelf, my Lord, the motives that decided him not to requeſt an audience when he came over in the character of Chargé des Affaires, with "*full powers to treat,*" as the public prints in the French intereſt had the audacity to aſſert on his arrival in 1793.—At all events your Lordſhip cannot be ignorant that he was eight days in this country, without offering, or even intending to deliver his credentials, until he received freſh inſtructions from Paris *. And if it had not been the object of France to deceive, delude, and finally attack this country, a conduct more conformable to juſtice, and to that decency and reſpect which are due from one nation to another, would certainly have been

* Vide The Conduct of France towards Great Britain, page 111, printed for G. Nicol, Pall Mall.

adopted,

adopted, and adhered to. It really, my
Lord, was not my intention to have faid fo
much, but I have been forced by the circumftances of the times to come more forward than I wifhed: not altogether from
motives of perfonal regard for the Minifter,
whofe talents I revere, and whofe wonderful powers of mind have twice faved the
empire*; but from that unbounded affec-
tion for my country, its laws, government,
and religion, which fuperfedes all other confiderations, and juftifies the zeal I have fhewn.
Minifters, however amiable and conciliating
their manners may be in the lefs turbulent
and more pleafing walks of private life—
with whatever dignity their public conduct
may be marked, and whatever advantages
may refult from the combined powers of
their wifdom, integrity, and exertions—
are, with all their virtues and qualifications,

* In refcuing the country from the dominion of
Faction, in 1784 and 1789.

but

but the atoms of an hour, hurried down the ftream of oblivion with other atoms, and doomed, like your Lordfhip and myfelf, to perifh! But the Britifh empire, and the Britifh conftitution—the pride, boaft, and fecurity of Englifhmen—the work of ages, and the admiration of the world—are, I truft, ETERNAL!

POSTSCRIPT.

I T was reasonable to expect that the multiplied excesses of the French would have convinced your Lordship of the danger of loosening those ligatures, by which men are held in peaceful and virtuous subjection to the dictates of reason, justice, and humanity. But example has lost its influence, and all the wholesome lessons of experience only serve to animate you, it seems, to a more decided and more violent opposition to their salutary suggestions:—every year, every day and hour—nay, my Lord, every minute teems with new and extraordinary events— every moment is pregnant with rude misshapen thoughts; the vile offspring of vice, folly, and irregular ambition, which, ripening into action, bid defiance to the sober

S   maxims

maxims of paſt and happier times, and aſſume a confidence that belongs excluſively to virtue. The ſavage cruelties of the untutored Indian are eclipſed by the ſtill more ſavage ferocity of the civilized European. The tomahawk and ſcalping-knife no longer excite horror, indignation, or ſurprife; while the wilds of America appear leſs terrible, and more ſecure, than the beſt cultivated and hitherto moſt poliſhed part of Europe. Not content with ſolitary individual ſacrifice, the French mow down each other by ſcores and hundreds; and that ſome idea may be formed of their extreme profligacy, the accuſed, when arraigned at the tribunal of perverted juſtice, impudently aſſert their claim to acquittal, not on their innocence, but on the multitude and enormity of their crimes *!—not on their pretenſions to character, or to the general good tenour of their behaviour, but on the

* Vide the defence of La Croix, and the remainder of that batch of aſſaſſins that were diſpatched.

uniform

uniform villany of their lives, paffed in the execrable purfuit of every thing that is infamous; and that the climax of iniquity fhould be perfect, we behold vice unabafhed taking rank of virtue; and on conviction, the abandoned remorfelefs herd founding their claim to pardon on the number of their crimes, and pleading their very guilt in the face of Heaven and the World, in bar of punifhment, and as a reafon why the blow of vindictive juftice fhould be arrefted —not enforced. And yet amidft thefe dreadful fcenes of riot, wafte, and devaftation!— of rapine, crime, and flaughter—amidft this univerfal carnage of the human race, we find tragedy converted into comedy, and murder made a paftime!—Paris abounds with balls, operas, and buffoons—For my part, I wonder that its wretched inhabitants can find time or appetite for dinner, much lefs a difpofition to mirth and feftivity; but their levity keeps pace with their barbarity, and they

have

have eighteen places of public diverſion conſtantly open beſides the Guillotine, which may be called the National Theatre (le Théâtre de la Nation) without a mockery of their woes or misfortunes.—Who can behold without affliction, the laws, manners, and dominion of a great Nation, a vaſt and ſplendid ruin!—Who can behold without horror, my Lord, the total deſtruction of the long eſtabliſhed habits, opinions, and urbanity of an entire people, once the object of our imitation, and at all times of our reſpect! And what image can the execrable horrors they inflict on each other, preſent to the aſtoniſhed and affrighted mind, but that of a wilderneſs of tigers, ſtimulated to fierce conflict by what alone inflames the brute creation to madneſs, and tearing each other to pieces with all the ferocity of their ſavage nature? And is it to this deplorable and degraded ſtate that your Lordſhip would reduce your happy and much envied country?

Is

Is it to enjoy a miferable and difhonoura-
ble triumph over its fubverted laws and
conftitution, that you pay court to the rep-
tiles, who, driven from houfe to houfe, and
expelled all decent reputable cover, affembled
in the fields laft week to flatter you into a
participation of their crimes, and feduce you
from that duty which you owe ftill more to
yourfelf, if poffible, than to your country?
Is it from the greafy exhalations of fuch beings, that your Lordfhip feeks for the unc-
tion that is to beatify and canonize you in
the opinion of pofterity? And is your ambition of fo fpungy a nature as to imbibe,
and hope to retain the noxious and fugitive
plaudits of a fenfelefs promifcuous rabble, on
the ftability of whofe fupport and affections
you can calculate with mathematical exact-
nefs, from the example of thofe who played
the fame game in France that your Lordfhip feems inclined to play in England; and
which it is our duty to prevent (fhould
the

[158]

the laws prove inadequate) by shaming you out of bad conduct and company, and forcing your intoxicated and bewildered mind to reflect on the direful consequences that must inevitably result to yourself, family, and name, by associating with men whose object is to throw the nation into confusion! My Lord, it behoves you to disavow their proceedings—It is incumbent on you to come forward with the dignity of an honest man, and reject the vote of thanks which they have had the insolence to propose, and which it would be infamy to accept—Your character is at stake—You must decide, not deliberate, or the world will think worse of your principles than it does of your understanding.

FINIS.

www.ingramcontent.com/pod-product-compliance
Lightning Source LLC
Chambersburg PA
CBHW020010030726
47500CB00002B/518